Morley Roberts, Cecil Roberts

Adrift in America

Or Work and Adventure in the States

Morley Roberts, Cecil Roberts

Adrift in America
Or Work and Adventure in the States

ISBN/EAN: 9783337338732

Printed in Europe, USA, Canada, Australia, Japan

Cover: Foto ©Andreas Hilbeck / pixelio.de

More available books at **www.hansebooks.com**

ADRIFT IN AMERICA,

OR

WORK AND ADVENTURE IN

THE STATES.

BY CECIL ROBERTS,

WITH AN APPENDIX BY

MORLEY ROBERTS.

LONDON:
LAWRENCE AND BULLEN,
169, NEW BOND STREET, W.
1891.

CONTENTS.

ADRIFT IN AMERICA.

CHAPTER I.

My New Departure.

I WAS not yet sixteen when I went to sea as an apprentice in the ship *Soukar*, 1,304 tons, belonging to Messrs. Shaw, Savill, and Company. During my four years' apprenticeship I was three times at Port Lyttelton, Christchurch, New Zealand, once in Melbourne, thence with coal to Anja Point, Java, which was afterwards destroyed by the great Krakatoa volcanic explosion. We received orders there for Rangoon, and at that port loaded rice for Europe. Leaving England again I went to Port Lyttelton once more, thence to Geelong, and being then out of my time I served as A.B. on the passage home.

My next voyage was in the barque *Bebington*, belonging to the same firm, as second mate. We went to Melbourne, thence to Timaru for orders, which sent us to Valparaiso, again for orders, which were now finally for Antofogasta, to load saltpetre. Thence we sailed for Queenstown and Hamburg, where I left the *Bebington*.

It was on returning home that my real adventures began, for though I saw enough hard weather and did a great deal of hard work in that five years, it was after all nothing more than comes in the course of learning his profession to every young seaman. And to tell the truth, I was pretty tired of the sea. It did not take me long as a youngster to learn to discount the romance of it, which lies chiefly either in ignorant imagination, or in the memory of some old salt who has forgotten the tough salt horse and weevilly biscuit to remember that he was then young and strong and able to enjoy himself when he got a rare chance. And apart from all romance there did not seem to be very much in the business. It was not only monotonous but poorly paid. So that is the reason why I made up my mind to go to America and see what could be done there. And if I did not succeed in making money, at any rate I had a very varied time and learnt something of the inside of a country.

When I landed in New York after a rather rough passage across the Atlantic I was in very good spirits, and thought I was going to do big things, though I had a very indistinct idea of how the big things were to be done. As a start, in company with a man called Mathews, who was on board the steamer in which I crossed the Atlantic, I went out to South Bend in the State of Indiana, where Mathews had a brother who owned a farm of three hundred acres.

Mathews' brother was building a barn that spring, and he was kind enough to give me a job "tending mason," or, as we should call it in England, mixing mortar and carrying a hod. It certainly staggered me a bit at first, but as nobody there seemed to think that there was anything *infra dig.* about it, I very soon came to look on it in the same way, and, with the rest of the people about there, to consider myself just as good as the President, even if I was not quite so clever. This job lasted about a month, after which Mathews engaged me as a farm hand for the rest of the summer at $15 a month, and I might have stayed there some time if I had been religious enough, or enough of a humbug to make people believe that I was, but being neither the one or the other, I soon got myself into bad odour and had to shift; for some of my actions and some of my yarns rather startled the saints about that part of the country, and consequently I got the cold shoulder right and left—no one would speak to me, and I was shunned as if I had the plague. One of my offences was that when I had occasion to speak of anybody's lower limbs, I called them legs, whereas the sanctified prudes about there always called them *limbs.* They considered legs indelicate I was told, but if all was

true that I heard I fancy that there were some of
the most disgusting hypocrites about that neighbourhood it has ever been my misfortune to come
in contact with.

I never did anything on purpose to irritate these
people, but nothing I could do was right, and I was
continually running against some snag in the shape
of an unwritten law which made things uncomfortable for me. On one occasion I had accepted
the invitation of two men (who were considered by
the religious part of the community to be two old
reprobates) to drive out to a place called Lakeville
one Sunday and go fishing. Now fishing of itself
was not considered to be a very objectionable
practice, but the man who indulged in the sport on
Sunday was considered as lost to all sense of moral
responsibility, and to be, at least until such time as
he had repented in sackcloth and ashes, on the
high road to destruction. The old fellows, both of
whom were what I should call very decent square-
dealing men, were quite different from each other
both in appearance and disposition, one being fat
and very fond of sitting down in a comfortable
place under a shady tree where he would put his
line in the water and sit for hours smoking and
blinking, quite content if he never got a bite, just
so long as nothing happened to make him exert
himself, while the other was a thin, wiry, energetic
kind of man who was everywhere and at everything,
continually on the move, and would not stay more

than a few minutes in one place unless he was catching fish or getting bites.

We went from Maple Grove to Lakeville in a conveyance that is called in the States a buck-board. On the way there a big rattlesnake came out of the fence at one side of the road and wriggling across our path got in amongst a pile of stones at the other side. Now in any country where snakes are plentiful most people are very anxious to kill as many of them as they can, not with any idea of lessening their number but from a feeling of hostility towards the whole race.

On seeing this particular snake we at once pulled up and the thin man, whose name was O'Brien, at once got down, and breaking a stick from some bushes that grew by the roadside, proceeded to try and dislodge him from his hiding-place in the pile of stones. However, the snake had either gone right through and out the other side, or at least would not come out again if he was still in there. This caused some delay, at which the other man, who had kept his seat in the buck-board, began to get fidgety, and I saw that he made two or three starts to say something but stopped himself. At length, losing patience, he said : " Now look here, O'Brien, what is it going to be, air we going a fishing, *or* air we going a snaking, because I want to know."

As we could not dislodge the snake we gave it up as a bad job and proceeded on our way. We had a very pleasant day, for which I got black looks for a week after. One of the men who took it upon himself to reprove me for what he called Sabbath-breaking, had said in my hearing, when told that his pigs were in a neighbour's clover field, "Oh, yes, I know they are, but I guess they are doing pretty well, and I believe I will let them stay there."

There is a kind of amusement in the backwoods known as a platform dance, and it was attending one of these affairs which finally put the "kibosh" on me as a possible member of Indiana backwoods society. A piece of land is cleared for this kind of dance out in the woods, and a raised dancing floor of boards is erected there. There is no roof over it, and, if by bad luck, it happens to rain, the festivities come suddenly to an end. The illuminations consist of candles in transparent Chinese lanterns, and the scene is often enough very pretty with a background of dark forest and the sky overhead. Some of the boys belonging to a neighbouring farm asked me to go to one, and as I thought it would be a change, I went. The company were mostly young people, though there was a sprinkling of older folks, and the dancing was of a very rough kind, mostly square dances for which the figures were called out by a man specially told off for the purpose. But no one in particular was "boss" of the entertainment, which was evidently run on the democratic principle of equal rights for every one. Every man brought a girl and many of them whiskey as well. Things went on very nicely until late at night, when most of the whiskey had been consumed, and one man wanted to dance with someone else's partner. This resulted in a fight and the combatants rolled off the platform. Some of their friends could not see a row without joining in, and with an accompaniment of yelling and screaming from the women, about half the crowd went to work fighting. Presently revolvers were drawn and a few shots fired, fortunately without hurting anybody, and this time the row ended without a coroner's inquest. Such entertainments do not always end so. The more sober ones of the party finally got the upper hand, and the drunken men were deprived of their weapons. We then thought it about time to go home. And it did not improve my character to have gone there.

One morning Mathews, who was a very good sort of a fellow—though as he had married into the respectable part of the community, he had to be like them—told me that he would pay me what he owed me, and that it would be best for me to clear out of that part of the country, as they had all come to the conclusion that I was not a fit person to associate with. I had been observed to chew tobacco, and it was also said that I had been seen coming out of a saloon one day that I was in town, both of which offences were, as I now found out, quite enough to stamp me as a bad man in that ultra-sanctified community, even if I had not gone fishing or dancing.

So pocketing Mathews' dollars and shaking the dust of Maple Grove from my feet, I proceeded on shanks's mare to South Bend, whither Mathews promised to send my baggage the next day.

It was in the month of August, and in Indiana the harvest was over or nearly so, with the exception of the corn, which is not picked till the first frost, so there was not much doing in the country and I did not care to stay in town, although I could have got work if I had wished for it. In fact I did get it in the Studebaker waggon works, but two days of such labour in a close room was enough for me, so I left my check on the board the second night and gave up working in a factory.

Where to go next was the question, and it was settled for me by Mathews' brother-in-law advising me to go to Dakota Territory, a place he described in very glowing colours. I have since thought that he was anxious to get me as far away as possible so that I should not come back in a hurry. However that may have been, the advice to go West was very acceptable to me, as it happened to fall in with my own wishes and ideas. So packing my baggage and paying my board bill, I went down to the depôt (railway station) and took a ticket for Fargo, which was then the largest city in Dakota. It was dark soon after we left South Bend, and some time about midnight I was landed at Chicago, in the Chicago and North-Western Railway depôt, to find that the train that I ought to have caught there had left, so I had to wait till twelve o'clock next day. My baggage being checked through to Fargo, I had no bother about that at the railway depôt.

I was very much struck with the comfort and convenience of the waiting rooms, which were supplied with beautiful rocking-chairs that made a tired man feel rested to look at. As money was not very plentiful with me at that time, I took possession of one of these, and slept there for the rest of the night, by that means saving hotel expenses.

In the morning I took a look round the city; of course I did not see much of the place, but what I did see gave me the impression that it was not a very beautiful city, though no doubt a very busy and prosperous one. It was here that I first saw cable cars in operation. The cables, of course, being out of sight, I was very much puzzled to make out what it was that was propelling the cars; at first I thought they were electric-motor cars, but I did not like to expose my ignorance to the public by asking any questions, so it was some time before 1 found out.

Down by the lake shore, the wharfs, at which were lying large numbers of schooners and also a good many large steamships, some of them apparently of as much as two and three thousand tons register, present the appearance of a seaport. This part of the city also has the same appearance as a corresponding part of any large seaport would have. The suits of oilskins and bundles of slop clothes, together with the strings of tin pots and plates that are seen hanging outside of dingy shops, which are presided over by greasy and persuasive-tongued Jews, give the place a regular briny look, and if I had not known that it was a thousand miles away from it, I might have fancied Lake Michigan a part of the real ocean.

However, I had not much time to gaze at anything, but had to hurry back to the depôt to catch my train. The scenery for the next part of my journey, viz., that part of it that lay through Illinois and Wisconsin, was not very striking, it being through dark forests of pine, hemlock, and spruce, in which the view was bounded by the line of trees on either side of the railway track; or, over open rolling prairies that were either under cultivation or covered with flocks and herds, and thickly dotted with homesteads, all of which looked very much the same. Sometimes, when the carriage was clear enough to do so, I lay down and slept. As we got up into Minnesota the country was more broken, and there were some very pretty lake scenes, this State being particularly remarkable for its lakes, though my route at this time did not take me through what may be called the lake district, which is in the north-eastern part of the State, where Lake Itasca, the source of the Mississippi, is situated. The nearest I ever was to this lake was when I was at Fargo, which is about 80 miles nearly west from it. It was early on Sunday morning when I arrived at St. Paul and found that I could not get a train on to Fargo till that night. As I was hungry and dusty and tired, I went on to an hotel and had a wash, some breakfast, and went to bed. But, somehow or other, I could not sleep, and was just thinking of getting up when I was startled by cries of fire. Jumping out of bed, I hastily donned some indispensable articles of clothing, and tucking the rest under my arm, and taking my boots in my hand, I bolted out of my room and ran downstairs. I had not gone far when I was met by a surging crowd of men, who were rushing to their rooms to rescue such property as they had left there, and they jostled me about and trod on my bare feet till I was glad to run into a room that I saw open and put my boots on. Thus equipped I managed to fight my way out into the street, where several fire engines were on hand ready for action. No one could see any fire or smoke, and it soon transpired that it was to some extent a false alarm. A gasoline cooking stove had exploded, but beyond scorching some of the cooks and spoiling a large quantity of food, no particular harm had been done. So after swearing for awhile over my sore toes, I went up to my room again and, dressing myself, I went out to see the city, for after that sleep was impossible.

The view of the Mississippi from the bluffs on which the upper part of the town stands is very fine; in fact, I think it is as fine a view as can be got on any part of the upper river. I do not remember anything else about the place that particularly impressed me, so I suppose there was not anything very striking to be seen, as I should have been sure to have noticed it if there had been.

As it was getting on towards evening, a large steamboat, a regular Mississippi steamboat, came to the landing, and as it was the largest boat that ran on the upper river, which is that part of it which is to the north of St. Louis, where it is joined by the Missouri, there was a large crowd down there to see it come in.

This was the first time that I ever saw a real Mississippi river boat, and it was a sight worth seeing; they are really very fine boats, splendidly fitted up, and very comfortable.

As I was standing looking at the crowd of nigger roustabouts discharging the cargo, a rather well-dressed and gentlemanly young fellow came up to me, and, saying " Good evening ! " asked me if I had seen a boat like that before. I told him that it was the first time that I had over seen either that river or a boat of that class. After some more conversation, he, according to the most approved transatlantic style, began to question me as to where I came from, where I was going to, and who

I was, and various other things that seemed to have a great interest for him. He then asked me if I had any job to go to at Fargo, and when I told him no, I was just going up there on "spec.," he asked me if I could drive horses, and I replied that I could.

"Look here, old man," said he, "I have got a job that will just suit you. I have a large general store in Fargo, and I want a man to drive a delivery waggon, and I think you would just suit me. There will not be much work to do, and I pay $40 a month and board. If you like to have the job, you can."

I thanked him for his offer, and accepted it at once. Now, although I was fresh in that country, I had quite enough experience of the ways of the world to be suspicious of a man's motives when he began to get too kind. So, as we walked up the street towards the "Planters' Hotel," where he said he was staying, I was waiting for him to come out with what he wanted. But he said nothing till we got up to the hotel, when he went into the office, and spoke a few words to the clerk. Then coming out to me, he said: "I have a large sum of money in the safe, but the proprietor is out, and has got the key with him. I have to pay the freight on some goods I am shipping to Fargo, and am short of $50; just lend it me, will you, and I can give it you back in the morning?" This was just the kind of request I had been expecting all along. So

I replied that I had no doubt of his honesty, but
that I did not make a practice of lending money to
perfect strangers.   Whereon he said, " Oh ! just as
you please.   I have no doubt I can get it from
someone else."   However, when he saw I was not
quite such a hay-seed as he had taken me for, he
sheered off, and I saw him no more.

It was now time to go down to the depôt, where
I accordingly went, and found the train that was
to take me on to Fargo was nearly ready to " pull
out," as the phrase goes in America ; so getting my
valise from the office, I jumped aboard, and made
myself as comfortable as I could for the night.
This part of my journey was done on the St. Paul,
Minneapolis, and Manitoba line, but what the
country was like I could not say, as it was dark up
to a few miles before we arrived at Fargo.   We
stopped for breakfast at a place called Moorhead.
The line here crosses the Red River of the North.
It is this river that gives the name to that district
known as the Red River Valley, although I never
saw anything resembling a valley in this perfectly
flat country.

A more uninteresting and thoroughly ugly town
I never saw than Fargo as it appeared when I first
saw it.   It was, like most other western cities, of
mushroom growth.   There were one or two large
wooden structures which they called hotels, and a
large number of second and third-rate boarding-
houses, also called hotels.   At one of these, the

" Park House," I put up, for I had no great amount of money, and wished to save it as much as I could till I could get something to do. I soon found that there was plenty of work to be got of a rough kind at fairly good wages; in fact, the supply of labour for the time being was not up to the demand, and so, of course, the labouring men were pretty independent. Everybody that had land there was anxious to get his thrashing done, and would give almost any wages to get men to go to work. It was not long before I was asked to go out and make one of a thrashing crew, but I said I had never done any of that kind of work, and did not know if I could manage it.

" Never mind," said the man, " you will make one, and we will find you something you can do. All I want is a man who will try to do what he is told." So as he was so anxious to get me, I agreed to go with him. It was to be $2 50c. a day, and board and constant work till the snow flew, if I liked to stay. The man who engaged me was in town expressly to get men, as some of his crew had left, and, as he termed it, "stuck him up," so he could not do a " darned thing " till he got some more to go out. He wanted four men, but could not get them, myself and one other being all he could find.

It was now about 12 o'clock in the day, and he wanted to get out to the farm that night in order to make a start in the morning. So going up to

the house, 1 rolled a few things I wanted in a
blanket, and giving the rest in charge of the boss
of the house, I was ready for the road.   When the
waggon came along I jumped in, and we started off
for the scene of our labours, which was about
10 miles out of Fargo.   Anything more dull,
dreary, and desolate-looking I can scarcely imagine
than the country through which we passed on this
journey.   The prairie was flat as a dish, and as far
as the eye could reach in every direction there was
nothing but stubble to be seen, blotched here and
there with black patches where piles of straw had
been burnt.   We passed two or three frame-houses
that sprang up out of the stubble, without a tree or
shrub or even as much as a fence round them; but
instead of enlivening the landscape, they seemed
only to make it look more dreary; for, weather-
cracked for the want of paint, with their staring
curtainless windows, they looked like so many
skulls stuck about on the prairie.

The waggon was heavily loaded and our progress
was slow, and as there was nothing to be seen of
any interest, and the others of the party were
engaged with their own thoughts, and kept silent,
the whole thing had such a depressing effect on my
spirits that I felt very miserable.

However, after about five hours of slow crawling,
we at last arrived in front of a large bare frame,
house which was the counterpart of those I had
already seen, and our journey was at an end.

The boss jumped down and began unhitching the horses, while some men that were about the place gave a hand to unload the waggon and carry the goods into the house.

I was told that there would be nothing for me to do that night, but that supper would be ready in a minute or two. I looked round to see if there was anything to wash at, but could not see anything of the kind about, so I inquired of one of the other men if there was any place where I could wash my face and hands. He looked at me and seemed rather surprised at my asking, and then drawled out, "You ain't dirty, I ain't washed this three days, I ain't got a towel of my own and they don't supply any here; but if you want to wash, there is a broken camp oven there, and there is some water in that cask (pointing out a barrel that stood at the side of the house), but if you ain't got soap of your own you won't get any here."

However, I had soap and a towel, so securing the broken camp oven and getting some water in it, I managed to wash. I had just finished when one of the men came out beating a tin plate and singing out " grub pile," which I was given to understand was the signal for supper. The whole crowd bolted into the house as if they had not had anything to eat for a week. The reason for this hurry, I soon found out, was that there was not room to seat everybody at once, so that two or three had to wait till someone else had finished, and then take his place. The consequence of this arrangement was that those that got left in the first rush generally came in for short commons, for if there was anything particularly nice on the table, that was gorged at once by the first crowd, and no one else ever got a show at it. Not being used to the place, and consequently not up to the move, I got left, and had to make my supper on bread and molasses and weak tea. Not being very hungry I did not care much about that, but one of the other fellows who got left was in a great state of mind about it, growling and cursing all the while he stigmatised the more fortunate part of the gang as a "lot of durned hogs" who were not fit to be amongst respectable people, by which I suppose he meant himself, although I soon found out he was a most outrageous glutton besides being a regular uncultivated savage in every other respect.

Supper being over, I made inquiries as to where we should sleep, and the man that had steered me up against the washing outfit, now informed me that it was not customary to provide any sleeping accommodation for a thrashing crew; "so" said he, "you must sleep where you can when you are on this kind of a racket, but this place is not bad, for there is room for all that are here to sleep in the stable, where there is plenty of good hay. At some places you have to hunt a roost in the straw stack, and if there comes any rain you are in a bad fix if there are not any waggon tilts on the place." On receiving this information I at once went for the structure that did duty for stable and general outhouse, determined not to get left on the sleeping part of the job as I had been on the supper.

The stable, or (as it is more generally called out West, or indeed in any part of the United States), the barn, had been constructed on the simple method of setting up a few posts to the height of eight or nine feet and putting some poles across for rafters and filling in the rest of the business by putting the straw carrier of the thrashing machine over it until the whole was thickly covered up with straw. This makes a fairly good temporary barn, and the method is much in favour in this part of the country.

I selected what appeared to me to be about the best spot for a roost, and taking a pile of hay and my blanket, I made a fairly comfortable bed. As I was pretty tired I lay down and was soon asleep. I did not enjoy my repose long before I was awakened by some more of the boys coming in and making their beds alongside of me. One of them remarked, "I think Dan might put his blamed mules the other end of the barn, they kept me awake half of last night and I don't sleep light neither." I began to wonder what Dan's mules might have been doing, but I was not left long in doubt about that, as about ten minutes afterwards those delightful animals made their appearance with a rush, and took up their quarters in the next stall to where we were lying. It immediately became apparent what was the trouble with them. Although there were two divisions in the manger, they both insisted on eating out of one, fighting and squealing continually. They would make a pause for a few minutes and then start in again with a shower of vicious kicks and squeals, and as this continued for the greater part of the night, I did not get much sleep.

It was barely daylight when we were awakened by the boss coming in and telling us that breakfast was ready, and we all accordingly turned out as we had turned in, namely, "all standing." Nobody seemed to care about washing but myself, but I made another application to the broken camp oven, and having given myself a bit of a smear, went in to breakfast. This meal was not much to brag about, strong, bitter, horribly tasting coffee, fried salt pork, and bread and a kind of composition they called butter, but heaven only knows what it really was.

Breakfast finished, I repaired to the barn where such of the men as had teams to drive were hitching their horses up. Dan was there with his mules. They were a really fine pair of animals, but vicious in the extreme. No mules that I ever saw were very gentle animals, but these were about the most infernal brutes that I ever set eyes on. When I arrived on the scene, Dan had succeeded in hitching up the near side one, but the off one stood with his head close up to the pole, being fast to the other mule by the neck yoke, with his hind quarters stuck out at an angle of ninety degrees from it, a position which he obstinately refused to alter, while he signified his disapproval of all attempts to make him move by savage squeals and whole showers of kicks discharged into space. After about 20 minutes of work they managed to get him into position by dint of shoving him with a long pole and pricking him with a pitchfork.

The whole crowd of us then started out for the place where the thrashing machine was set. None of the wheat was stacked, but just stood in the shock, and had to be loaded on to waggons, and hauled to the machine. As I had not been at the work before, they put me to pitching the sheaves up on to the waggons, this being the work which required least experience. This work was rather severe and soon made me very tired. This job is hardest on the wrists, and mine soon became so sore that I had to tell the boss that I could not do any more of it, on which he set me to cut bands on the machine This work was a great deal easier than the other, but the dust nearly choked and blinded me. However, I stayed at it for five days, but by that time my eyes were so sore on account of always being full of dust that I told the boss I could stand it no longer and would leave. So he gave me a check for my money and an intimation that if I stayed there any longer he should charge me a dollar a day for my board.

Next morning I rolled up my blankets and started for Fargo on foot. This was about my first experience of bonâ fide tramping, of which I was later on to do so much. The distance was only about 10 or 12 miles, but the roads were very bad in parts, and here I may put in a word or two about roads in this part of the country. The method of making them is simple in the extreme, though it can scarcely be called efficacious, and consists in simply ploughing up a strip of land the width it is intended to make the road, dragging it down with a harrow, and then leaving the traffic to do the rest. If just after the road is made there happens to come a spell of rainy weather, the whole affair is soon reduced to a quagmire, and the consequence of this is that people drive out on the sides of the road in search of firmer ground, thus making another road which in its turn is reduced to the same condition as the original one. In some places where there was a depression in the prarie, I have seen as many as seven or eight tracks of this kind, all churned up into a ditch of mud. This kind of thing renders it necessary for a foot passenger to make a wide circuit to avoid the mud, and then if he is not remarkably careful he will get in over his knees, as indeed I myself did on more than one occasion during this walk. And the condition of these roads

is altered but not greatly improved by a continued
spell of fine weather, as the soil here is largely
mixed with a kind of blue clay, locally known as
"gumbo." Now, the roads being first cut up into
ruts in rainy weather, cake to the hardness of a
brick in that shape, so that when dry they are
really dangerous to travel on, especially in the
dark.

But to return to my tramp. I walked on lively
enough for the first two or three miles, but after a
bit the roughness of the roads began to tell on me
as I was not used to much walking at that time.
Up to noon I had covered about half the distance to
Fargo, and was pretty well fagged out. I then
began to try to shorten the distance by cutting
across the stubble, and by this means soon got so
completely lost as not to have the least idea which
way I was going. This would not have happened
to me only the sky, which had been quite clear in
the morning, had now become overcast, and I could
not see the sun. I kept tramping on in uncertainty
as to whether I was going to Fargo, or away from
it, though it was now beginning to get dusk, and
the rain, which had been threatening since noon,
began to fall in large drops which promised well for
a good downpour before long. I now came into
sight of a small house built of sods cut from the
prairie, which I had not been able to see at a distance
on account of its looking more like a mound of earth
than a house.

My spirits, which had been down to zero, now began to rise and I started for the house, being pretty sure of getting either shelter for the night or directions as to my way on to Fargo. However, when I got to the door I saw a tousled looking young woman and three or four half-naked children inside, all of whom seemed to regard me with, anything but friendly feelings. The woman jumped up and banged the door .in my face, and fastened it on the inside, and all I could do would not induce her to open it again. But she opened a window and motioned me to go away, and spoke in some language I could not understand, but which, I think, was Norwegian or Swedish. Seeing that there was no hope of shelter or information here, I started off again. It was now getting quite dark and the rain was falling heavily. I was certainly in a fix, and I could see nothing for it but a night on the open prairie in the rain. It was anything but a pleasant prospect. However, just as I had made up my mind that there was no chance of anything else but to stay out in the open all night, I caught sight of a bright light in the distance which I at once recognised as the electric light on the big tower at Fargo, and which I had heard could be seen for a distance of 20 miles across the prairie in clear weather. I at once struck out for the light, going over everything in my way. I was completely fagged out by this time, and could scarcely drag one leg after the other. The rain was making the ground muddy and slippery, and as it was pitch dark I kept falling over obstacles that I could not see, and slipping and stumbling into mud-holes until I was bruised and plastered with mud from head to foot.

I now could see by the increasing number of lights that I was getting close to the city, and I began to feel in better feather, when all at once I went over head and ears into a slough, a long narrow stretch of water formed by a depression in the prairie, which in this instance was stagnant and stinking. After floundering about for some minutes I crawled out on the right side, nearly blinded and stifled by the filthy water, some of which I had swallowed.

A few hundred yards more put me in the main street at Fargo, and a more wretched and bedevilled object probably never landed there since the first house was built.

It being about midnight and raining, there were not very many people about, and every one had turned in at the Park House, the place where I had been staying when I was in Fargo before, and where I had left my traps. It took me about a quarter of an hour hammering at the door before I could get in, and some time more before I could get at my trunk to get out a change of clothes. The night porter was inclined to be surly at first on account of getting his nap spoiled, but when he saw the condition I was in he relented and gave me all the help he could, and procured me some whiskey which

he said would do me good; although it nearly
poisoned me, I' was glad to get it, as it seemed to
put some life into me, and seemed to help warm
me a bit. After getting shifted I turned in and
was soon asleep, and so ended my first attempt at
making a living in Dakota.

CHAPTER II.

Winter on Maple River.

After my long walk I slept rather late next morning, and should have slept later still if it had not been the custom of the house to have everybody out of bed before nine a.m. whether he liked it or not. There were a few who escaped the general turning out, but these were "bad men" who, when anyone knocked at their doors, blasphemed horribly, and threw out dark hints about six-shooters and Winchester rifles. These worthies were left to themselves, and turned out when they liked, did just what they liked, got their breakfast when any other man would have been told that he could only have it at the appointed time, and if that did not suit him he could get out. I could have very well slept for an hour or two more, and if I had known that posing as a desperado would have gained me that privilege, I should certainly have done so, but as it was I turned out grumbling.

I was now once more out of a job, and altogether too stiff and sore to care about looking for one that day. So I sat in the verandah and rested myself in an easy chair, and treated every offer of work with scorn. I sent several would-be employers of labour away predicting that the day was not far distant when they would see every lazy blackguard in the town starving.

The next morning the proprietor of the house came to me and asked me if I would take the job of "clerk," as the man who was at that time occupying that position was going to leave. As far as I could judge the work attached to the job was not very hard, so I accepted his offer and started in on my new duties at once. I found that clerk was merely a name, as there were no duties to perform which required anything more than the simplest knowledge of reading and writing, and scarcely that.

I was first of all required to sweep out the office, *i.e.*, the common room of the hotel, next to go into the back yard and chop firewood for the cook; this took me up till dinner time, and then I got a spell for an hour or two. In the evening I had again to sweep out the office and repair to the back yard to make sure that there was wood enough chopped to go on with next morning. It was also part of my duty to go out at meal times and ring the bell in the middle of the sidewalk.

In the evening of the first day I made the discovery that it was also considered part of my duty to take all the drunken men to bed; this was a very bad job indeed, and one of considerable danger at times when I got hold of a rough customer.

I went on with this job for about three days, and was just about full of it—indeed I had made up my mind to give the boss notice to find another man—when a man named Beaver came there to stay the night. Business happened to be slack at the time, and I got into conversation with him. I found that he was more than usually intelligent, and, as far as I could judge, seemed to be rather a nice fellow. He asked me how I liked my job, and on my answering not at all, he offered to take me out on his farm, which lay about 40 miles west of Fargo, near a place called Castleton. I at once consented, and as we soon came to terms as to wages, I once more changed my occupation to that of a farmer.

I squared up accounts with the boss of the hotel, and next morning, in company with my new boss, set off for Castleton.

There was no regular passenger train running that morning, so we went on what is called an "accommodation," that is, a freight train with a passenger car at the end of it. The road-bed was not in very good condition; we were continually stopping to put out and pick up cars, and our progress was slow. We stayed on a siding out in the middle of the prairie for nearly an hour to let the east-bound mail pass us. Owing to the slow progress we made, it was pretty well on in the afternoon when we arrived at Castleton. This place was merely a clump of frame-houses with a church and a bank, and a couple of hotels, and about 1,500 inhabitants, but was considered a town of considerable importance.

It being too late to go out to the farm that night, Beaver put me into one of the hotels, and went home himself, as he had a house there where his wife kept boarders. My night at this place was enlivened by a free fight, which started just as I had gone to bed. As far as I could find out the row was the outcome of whiskey drinking. Two of the men who were taking a leading part in the row were thrown out into the back yard to finish their quarrel by themselves, and there one of them was found next morning with his brains knocked out. The weapon with which it had been done was a spade. The other fellow had made himself scarce, and, as far as I ever heard, was never caught.

After breakfast next morning Beaver, whom for the future I shall call Hank, put in an appearance with a waggon and a pair of horses, and we started for his farm, which was situated on the Maple River about eight miles away from Castleton. As the waggon was heavily loaded, and we had to go at a walking pace, it was well on in the afternoon when we arrived at our journey's end.

This place requires no description, as it was the counterpart of the other place I was at thrashing, only not quite so big. We had two days of thrashing to do here, and after that was over I was put to ploughing with a sulky plough. This was a job that suited me better than anything I had struck since coming up to Dakota.

But although I liked the job of ploughing well enough, I met with an adventure after being at it for a few days that came very near costing me my life, or at the least some broken bones. The way of it was this:—There is a kind of weed very plentiful in this part of the country which is commonly called the tumble weed; what its right name is I do not know. The peculiarity of this weed is that it grows on a very small stem, but branches out at the top into the shape of a ball and often grows to a very large size. In the fall of the year these weeds die and dry up, but unlike most other kinds of weeds, they do not stay where they die, but break off close to the ground, and the wind rolls them over and over, and being very light the slightest breeze will send them skipping and jumping across the prairie like a herd of deer or antelopes, for which they are often taken by people fresh to the country. On the occasion of which I am now speaking I was driving four horses in what is called a gang plough, that is a plough with two shares, so constructed that the ploughman rides on the plough instead of walking behind it. The ploughshares are manipulated by means of a lever. It may be necessary to mention that the horses used for this job are not the same as are used for ploughing in England, but a kind of light coach horse which will do just as good work between the shafts of a buggy or as a saddle hack as it will in the plough. It was about the middle of the forenoon, when the team was comparatively fresh, that a lot of these tumble weeds came jumping and frolicking one over the other like a herd of some curious kind of animals, and two or three of the largest stuck in between the legs of my leaders, which unfortunately were a pair of skittish and half-broken colts. I could see at once that I was going to have a bolt, so I took hold of the lever, and, throwing the plough out, settled myself firmly in my seat to try and guide the team over the smoothest ground, and if possible avert a smash. In about half a minute I was flying across the prairie at nearly racing speed, for the horses were thoroughly frightened, and the more they galloped the more they seemed to me to scare themselves. The plough being a light kind, and much like a sulky, danced and jumped about in such a manner as to make it a very difficult matter indeed for me to keep my seat, let alone guide the horses. However, I managed somehow or other to keep them clear of any serious obstacle, till, after a gallop of about three miles, they pulled up of their own accord, but not till they were regularly played out and not much good for work for the rest of that morning. After this mishap Hank decided not to use the gang plough any more but to use two single-furrow sulkies with three horses each. I forgot to mention that Hank one evening gave me a rifle and a lot of cartridges, and sent me on a fool's errand to shoot tumble weeds, which he said were antelope. I walked some considerable distance before I found out the trick that had been played me.

Some time in the summer, and before I came up to that part of the country, Hank had bought the right to cut the hay on a school section. This hay was now standing in three large stacks in the middle of this section. I may as well explain, for the benefit of those who do not know, that a school section is a section of land, *i.e.*, a square mile, set apart by the Government for the purpose of raising funds for building and maintaining schools. There was an old man living a few miles from us whose name was Gallagher, who owned about twenty scrub colts, which he used to let run wild in defiance of the law and to the great annoyance of everyone in the neighbourhood. Most people at one time or other had suffered loss through these animals, but did not like to kick up a row about it for fear of appearing unneighbourly. These beasts had lately been tearing down Hank's hay stacks, and he had sent me with a horse to drive them away, which I had done several times, but they always came back again. Of course it was not likely that Hank was going to stand the loss and destruction of his hay, and it was quite out of the question to keep a man, that he was paying wages to and wanted for other work, continually running after another man's horses. He had told Gallagher about it once or twice, but to no purpose; so one Sunday morning, when we saw the old fellow riding down the road, Hank jumped up and said to me, "Now, you come along and hear what this old cuss has got to say about those colts of his." When he came up to us he stopped, and Hank in a very temperate manner put the case before him, saying that, much as he regretted the necessity, if something was not done at once to stop the depredations that were being committed on his hay stacks, he should have to take proceedings at law to recover the damage.

At this Gallagher took rather high ground, and, trying to run a bluff on Hank, said, "You can't do that, you know, for there is no law on a school section."

"Oh," said Hank, "no law on a school section; are you quite sure of that?"

"Quite," said he. "I have known of several cases where it has been tried, but it was always decided the same way."

"Very good," said Hank, turning to me; "now we know that there is no law to stop a man from doing what he likes on a school section, you and I will take our rifles and shoot those darned colts as soon as we have had our dinner."

This view of the case had never struck old Gallagher, and completely staggered him, so that

he promised to see to the matter, and this time he
kept his promise, which was a very good thing for
his colts, though if he had not done so the job of
shooting them would have been a little break in the
monotony of farm labour.

There was one other man working on Hank
Beaver's place besides myself, and for a long time
we were both at this same job of ploughing which
was my usual work; he ran one plough and I the
other, and we both had three horses to look after.
After we had finished Hank's own land he put us
to ploughing for the neighbours, he taking the
contract at so much an acre.

This work was very pleasant as long as the
weather was fine, but when the frosts began to
come in it got to be very cold and miserable. We
ploughed up to the tenth day of November. On the
morning of that day I went out as usual muffled
up in a buffalo overcoat and long boots, with my
head in a big fur cap. I made two or three
unsuccessful attempts to get the plough point into
the hard frozen ground, but seeing it was no good
I gave it up for a bad job, and went back to the
house.

We then put the ploughs in a shed after greasing
all the working parts, returned the horses to the
stable, and set to work to prepare the house for the
coming hard weather. This is rather a peculiar,
and to a stranger, rather a disgusting job, and

consists in banking the house up all round with stable manure. If there is enough manure this is done to a thickness of several feet, and as high up as the eaves. After finishing this job there was not much we could do, as the weather became more and more severe every day.

As there was not any work of a profitable nature being carried on, Hank could not afford to pay any great amount of wages, so he offered to give me $10 a month to stay and look after the place during the winter. This does not seem much, but in reality it was a very liberal offer, for many people in that country in the winter are glad to get a job to work for their board instead of paying for it, as they would otherwise have to do. Seeing nothing better, I closed with his offer, and prepared to put the winter in as comfortably as circumstances would permit.

Now Hank had a wife and a fairly comfortable house in Castleton, so it was not to be expected that he should stay out on the farm when there was nothing more to be done, as he had a man there whom he could trust to look after the place. So in a day or two after it had frozen up, he hitched up a team, and put on a load of hay to take to his place in town, where he kept a cow. He left plenty of everything in the way of provisions in the house, enough to last me all the winter, and I had a running order on the store at a place called Durban, on the St. Paul, Minneapolis, and Manitoba

line which was situated about five miles away. All
the work I had to do was to feed and water four
horses and two bullocks, and clean the stable out
when the weather was sufficiently mild to allow me
to do so. This, together with cooking my own
grub, was all I had to do, and before the finish I
found it too little.

There was nothing at all in the house to read,
and when the weather was too bad for me to get
out I spent all the time I could sleeping ; but this
resource soon failed me, and I was sometimes
nearly melancholy mad, although some days the
weather would be beautifully fine, without a breath
of wind, the sky a clear blue, and the air so clear
and transparent that things miles off across the
prairie looked quite near.

There was not much for me to hunt, the jack-
rabbit being the only thing there was to be got.
The word jack as applied to rabbit is a contraction
of jackass-rabbit, given them on account of their
long ears and large size generally. It is rather a
hard thing to shoot these fellows after the snow
flies, as they turn quite white. They are not at all
timid, and on more than one occasion I got quite
close to one, and all I could see of him was a pair
of pink eyes staring at me out of the snow, then
before I could realise that it was a rabbit and get
my gun on it, away it would whisk across the
prairie, scattering a small cloud of frozen snow
in its wake, and leave me to go and look for

another, to be served in the same way when I found him.

There was also a kind of prairie fowl very plentiful about here which the people called grouse. These birds were very easy to shoot as they would roost in some of the low stunted bushes that grew in places along the banks of the Maple River, sometimes as many as 15 or 20 in a bunch. The report of a gun would not frighten them a bit, and they would sit there until I had shot the whole lot. I soon got tired of this kind of hunting, and should never have troubled after any more of them, only they were good eating, and I used to keep a supply on that account.

After he had been in town about a week, Hank put in an appearance again one afternoon; he had come up to see how I was getting on and to haul in another load of hay. It was very lucky for him that he came that day instead of the next, as about noon on the next day, and that would have been about the time when he would have been half-way on his journey, one of those storms known in Dakota and the western countries as a blizzard, started in and stayed with us for three days. This one was the first thing of the sort I have ever seen, though I had often heard and read about them. The reality was so much worse than anything I had ever imagined, that I thought it was a more than commonly bad one. On my telling Hank so he laughed, and said it was quite an ordinary one. As

I said before, it started about noon; we were sitting down to dinner when all at once the sun, which had been shining brightly, became obscured, and though we were in a warm house with a large stove red hot, we at once became sensible of a lowering in the temperature. Hank jumped up, and going to the window looked out and remarked, " she's here." " Who's here ?" said I. " A blizzard," he answered. As he spoke it was on us, with a peculiarly dreary kind of wailing sound, and the air was at once as dark as midnight. The snow was not falling, but was being driven along in a line with the earth by the wind, which was now blowing almost a hurricane. The snow was not what people in Europe generally see, but more like finely powdered glass, which stuck to and froze fast on anything it touched.

There had been an old breaking plough left just outside the house, and Hank said, it must be moved at once, or it would raise a snowdrift that would bury up the door yards deep, and, when it was once started, perhaps the whole house. The thing being only a few yards away, I was going to run out and just move it, and come back again. But Hank said, " Just you stop a bit; don't go and commit suicide." He then told me to put on my wool-lined rubber boots and a big overcoat, also to wrap up my ears carefully. He then got a long line, and tied it round my waist, and seeing that I had no gloves on, made me put them on at once.

" For," said he, " if you go out and catch hold of any of the ironwork about that plough with bare hands, you would have the flesh taken clean off to the bone, just as if you had taken hold of a piece of red hot iron."

All being now ready, we went to the door. And Hank said, " Just you run out, and throw the plough round the corner of the house, and then follow the line back to the house. If you cannot find the plough, do not stay long, but come back at once." I was quite sure I knew where it was, and, opening the door, I made a bolt out to get it, but, after groping about for a minute or two, I was glad to go back to the house. All the hair that showed under the rim of my fur cap was full of frozen snow, and my face smarted as if it had been scalded. I made two more attempts before I finally stumbled across the plough and put it out of the way. When I got back to the house again I felt as if every particle of warmth had been extracted from my body, and my fur cap and buffalo overcoat were both coated with frozen snow, so that I looked like an image of Father Christmas. Hank shoved me in the back room, where there was no stove, for me to warm up by degrees. A nice place to warm in certainly, when the thermometer stood 25° below zero there, and a half bullock that was hanging there was frozen so hard that we could scarcely hack a piece off with a felling axe.

The blizzard lasted till the afternoon of the third day, and during that time, of course, we could not leave the house for anything. On the morning of the second day, on going into the back room, which was on the weather side of the house, we found it about a quarter full of snow, the whole of it having come in through a crevice in a corner of the window-frame that had been overlooked when we were filling up the chinks. This was no bigger than an ordinary keyhole, but in those few hours it had let in nearly a ton of snow, and would have let in a great deal more if it had been higher up, as it only stopped when the snow on the inside came to the level of the hole and plugged it up. On the afternoon of the third day, when the storm let up, Hank and I went out to survey the premises, and found the barn where the horses and bullocks were converted into, or rather covered by, a small mountain of snow. We at once proceeded to dig the door out, to give the poor beasts some water and hay. This we did not accomplish that night, and next morning, when we got the stable door open, we had another job as big to dig out one side of a haystack.

Long before we could get the stable door open we could hear the horses whinnying when they heard us coming, but when we got the door open their joy knew no bounds; it was worth all the work just to see how pleased they were at the prospect of getting a feed and a drink of water.

They would not eat anything till they had water, and, as they would not touch the frozen snow, we had to cut a hole in the ice, which was no small job, as it was frozen several feet thick. We used to melt snow for our own use, but it was too long a process to be any good for watering the cattle.

After a day or two Hank went back to Castleton with another load of hay, and I was once more left to my own devices.

A favourite amusement of mine at this time, when the weather was mild enough to allow me do it, was to go out in the morning and cut holes in the ice. The musk-rats would then come out, and, as I came back to the house, wherever I found a track from a hole, I used to follow it up till I saw the rat, and then run him down and kill him with a club. It is a very easy matter to run them down, as they are not at all quick when they are once out of the water, though smart enough when in it. Their skins are worth from 15 to 25 cents each, according to size and quality. I had some traps as well, but did not have much luck with them.

After what I had seen of the blizzard, I was frightened to go far away from the house for fear of another one coming on, as there is always a danger of one at any minute, and if it catches a man any distance from a place of shelter, it is ten to one he will be frozen to death, and no one know where he is till the crows find him when the snow melts in the spring.

There was now another thing that began to be annoying, and that was the wolves howling round the house at night. About two weeks before it froze up we had a mare taken sick, and when she died we buried her at the back of the barn, and now the wolves used to come every night and try to dig her up, and the snapping and snarling, varied by a howl, first from one and then from another, then a full chorus from the whole pack, was about as dismal and eerie a sound as I have ever chanced to hear. I have heard it said that frost destroys scent, but that is all rubbish, or how did the wolves know that the mare was buried there when the ground was frozen so hard that I could not drive the point of a pickaxe into it more than about an inch at a time? I put up with the noise for a night or two, thinking they would give it up as a bad job; but not a bit of it; they meant to have that mare, or die there themselves.

So being about tired of their music, I made up my mind to try and stop it. The night when I came to this resolution was beautifully clear, with a full moon, and besides that the northern lights made it nearly as light as day. I turned in as usual, after filling the stove up to the top and putting the damper on, so it would burn till morning. I had not been long turned in, and was thinking what a fool I was to be in such a position, when up started the concert again. I was feeling dismal enough before, but this put the set on my temper properly. So out of bed I jumped, and getting into my clothes, I went for my Winchester rifle, and going up to the top room—I was afraid to open the shutters of the lower window for fear they might try to get in—and opening the window, I started to knock them over. There were seven there, and they stood till I had shot the last one. They did not seem to know or care what was happening to them. I have read and heard it said, that if one wolf out of a pack is shot, the others will eat him; however, these did not attempt to do anything of the sort. As no more put in an appearance that night, I had a bit of a quiet spell of it. The next morning I went out and tried to skin one, but he was frozen as hard as a rock; so I just left them there; and although wolves used to be round every night and sometimes in the day, I never saw that they tried to eat any of the dead ones.

It was now well on in December and the winter was in full swing, but as there was about four months more of it to come, I began to think I had made a rather foolish arrangement by deciding to spend it in Dakota. My mind began to dwell on what I had heard about New Mexico and Texas and California, and I determined that when Hank came out again I would make a shift to a more genial climate. It was nearly a week before he put in an appearance, during which time my life went on as usual, and I got more and more lonely and thoroughly made up my mind to get away on the first opportunity.

At last one day Hank turned up, and I told him that I would settle up and leave the country. He tried to dissuade me from going, and said it was very foolish to make a move at that time of the year, and it would have been well for me if I had listened to him, but my mind was made up, and south I would go in spite of all he could say to me. Seeing it was no use to talk to me he gave me what he owed me, which together with what I had, made about $90, not a great deal to start out on in the dead of winter in a strange country; but I had made up my mind to go, and go I would in spite of everything. So when Hank went in I went in with him, taking my things along with me. I began to find that to travel in America one must travel light, so I got rid of my trunk and packed just what I thought I needed in a valise, and that, with a Winchester rifle and a cartridge belt, was all my baggage.

When we got into Castleton it was too late for the east bound mail and there was no train till the next day. I stayed that night at Hank's house and all the next day, as the train was not due till late in the afternoon. He still tried to persuade me to stay and go back to the farm, but it was no good. I was bound south, so I bade him good-bye.

CHAPTER III.

South towards Santa Fé.

Of my journey from Castleton down to St. Paul
I know nothing, as it was dark all the way till just
before we got to St. Paul. I had only taken a
ticket as far as there, as I heard that various
railway companies were cutting rates and that there
would be a chance of a cheap ride for perhaps as
far as I wanted to go. However, in this I was
disappointed, and I had to pay the full fare. I
went from here to Omaha in Nebraska, but do not
remember a great deal about the journey except
that, although there was no snow or frost, it was
continually raining. Every place we passed was
deluged with mud, and all the inhabitants appeared
to have been damp so long that they were going
mouldy. In fact, the whole face of the country
seemed to be bleared over and everything was in a
very moist and uncomfortable condition.

All this was very depressing; I felt very
miserable and began to suspect that I had made
a fool of myself by being in such a hurry to
leave a place where I was well off and sure of a
job as long as I liked to stay. The state of

my purse, too, was not as satisfactory as it might have been, and I began to see that railway travelling was rather more expensive than I had reckoned on.

It was about 9 or 10 a.m. when I arrived in Council Bluffs ; it was raining steadily and everything had a steamy and generally uncomfortable look. It was here, looking from the window of the car as we crossed the bridge that spans it and connects Council Bluffs with Omaha, that I first saw the Missouri River. It was not by any means a lively sight. A mighty river doubtless, but it looked to me also a mighty dirty one ; the water was the colour of yellow ochre and I could see things that appeared to be snags sticking up in two or three places.

Arriving in Omaha I left my valise in the depôt and had a look round the town, but could not see anything that at all enticed me to stay. I went to two or three employment agencies, but could come at nothing satisfactory, so I determined to push away further south at once before my money was all done. I went round to all the railroad ticket agents, called scalpers, in the city, and at last decided to go down as far as Topeka in Kansas, as that was the cheapest journey I could pick out for the distance. After paying for the ticket I had still about 15 dollars left. It was not much to me in my then state of ignorance with regard to making money spin out, but enough to have taken me across the continent if I had known as much about travelling as I was soon to learn.

When I arrived at Topeka, which is the capital city of Kansas, the sun was shining, there had been no rain there lately and the place looked quite cheerful. My spirits began to rise again and I determined to make a stay and see if there was anything in the way of work to be obtained. I went round the town to have a look for a cheap place to stay at, and finding one suited to my means down by the Atchison, Topeka, and Santa Fé railway depôt took up my quarters there. Even this place, which was only a dollar a day house, would, I knew, be too expensive a place for me to stay at very long unless I could get something to do pretty soon. I rustled round but could not get a job, as things were very slack at that particular time of the year.

The house I was staying at being near to the depôt and a cheap place, was much frequented by train men, particularly brakesmen; one of these was rather a nice fellow and I struck up an acquaintance with him. In the course of conversation one day he advised me to go further west, as he said I should stand more chance of getting something to do there than if I stayed in Topeka. On my saying that I had no money to spend in railway travelling, he looked at me in a rather surprised way and said, " Well, you certainly must be green to pay away your money to railroad

companies when you can travel for nothing if you
. like."

"Travel for nothing?" said I ? "What do you
mean?"

"Why," replied he, "just go down to the freight
yards and find out when there is a train going your
way, and get into a box car and keep quiet till the
train starts. You will get a bit of a lift on your
journey even if they find you and put you off at the
first stop. And then all you have to do is to wait
till another train comes along, get on to it, travel as
far as you can, and then take another, and so on
till you get to the end of your journey. You will
soon pick it up, and you will meet lots of men
doing the same thing who will put you up to all
the dodges. I tell you it is a long way ahead of
paying your fare : just you try it!"

"But," said I, "how about my baggage?"

"Oh! that's all right," he said, "express it to
the place you are going to, and when you get there
all you have to do is just to go and get it."

He then offered to take me down to the yards
any night I wanted to go, and told me a great deal
about "beating" which was then quite new to me.

For to beat one's way, or to beat the conductor
or the railroad, are equivalent phrases for travelling
in the cars without paying any fare, and it is the
usual means by which the wandering tramp, who
has seldom any great liking for actual tramping,
shifts his quarters from some undesirable locality

where food is scarce and people unkind to another, where he hopes to find things better from his point of view. As he is not only a bird of passage, but a bird who prefers a country where it is moderately warm at nights, the same man will sometimes spend his summer in Montana or Dakota, and luxuriously winter in warmer Mexico or Southern California, and the thousands of miles which intervene he dexterously accomplishes by beating his way. As a matter of fact, it is not only the professional tramp who cheats the railroad, though to be sure he is the most skilful hand at it, but any one of enterprise without money who finds it necessary to do a long piece of travel in some emergency. I acknowledge "the corn" myself, as they say across the Atlantic, and I owe no few dollars to the various railroads of the United States. But to get to particulars, which I learnt afterwards, for I was green enough at this time.

There are many ways of avoiding payment both on freight and passenger trains. To travel constantly by an express passenger is a kind of blue ribbon among tramps, and there are some far too proud to condescend to a freight train, which they leave to the more humble-minded and less daring of their brethren. As to methods, there are two chief ones, the first the "Universal Ticket," and the other "Jumping the Blind Baggage." These expressions would convey no meaning at all to most people even in America unless they happened to be acquainted with these methods of travel and the phraseology of the men who make a kind of profession of them. The universal ticket is a board, with some notches cut in it to fit the iron stays running underneath the carriages, and on this seat the tramp sits in a crouching attitude while the dust whirls about him as the train runs from one stopping place to another. The time chosen is almost invariably night, and it is no uncommon thing to see the conductor go along the train and look with his lamp for such unauthorised travellers. But these birds are too downy to be caught with such chaff; they hop off the moment the train stops, get into the darkness on one side, and the moment the train starts they jump out as quick as lightning, fix their board again, and go ahead once more. The " Blind Baggage Racket" is to get on the baggage car, which has a door at one end only. The end without a door nearest the locomotive is technically termed blind, and the tramp will sit there quite at his ease until the train slows up. As soon as it does he is off and hides, and only gets on again when it is in motion. I heard of a wooden-legged man who was the smartest hand ever known at this trick.

Another method which works equally well on both passenger and freight trains is to get on the engine just above the pilot, or cow-catcher, underneath the great head-light, which forms such a noticeable feature of American engines at night. This light is so blinding that it is hard to see if anyone is there or not, and often a tramp can get a lift of a hundred miles without moving from his seat. Then if he is seen and has to get off, all he has to do is to wait for the next train, and jump that. A man whom I knew, who was knocking about America in much the same way I did myself, was once ignominiously ejected from a freight train in New Mexico. He said nothing, but waited for the passenger express, jumped the blind baggage, and went past the freight train as it lay side-tracked, and when it came in at the station to which he had been bound, he was seated on a box on the platform kicking his heels. "Hullo! young fellow," said the brakesman, "how did you come here?" "Oh," said he, "I was too tony," (high-toned, proud) "to come on a freight. I came on the Thunderbolt."

But most beating is done on freights as they are so much easier, and most tramps prefer to get in a closed car, a box car as it is called there, or, as they humorously express it, a " side-door Pullman." These cars have a sliding door in each side, and a little door at each end. When the train is composed mainly of empty cars, the doors are often open, and never sealed, hence it is easy enough to get into them. But when they are full the little end doors are usually bolted, and the side doors sealed with a little leaden button or tag. It is an indictable offence to break these, and it requires

some experience and ingenuity to get into a car
without doing so. Yet even that is to be done
with care. The tramp selects his car as it stands
in the yard before the train is made up, and taking
a fish-plate he uses it as a lever to shift the door
from its runners, and crawls in. Going to the
end of the car he unbolts the little door, gets out,
replaces the main door, gets in through the small
one again, bolts it, and is safe, for none can see it
has been tampered with, and no one can enter
it without going through the same manœuvres
himself. He is safe then until the car reaches
its destination. However, this is so difficult and
complicated a task that few undertake it, and most
are content to hunt for an unbolted end door, for it
is nearly certain there will be one left so through
carelessness. The brakesmen are continually on the
look out for tramps, not always with the design of
making them set off, but in order that they may
" put up the stuff," in other words, give them
something to allow them to ride. A few are so
soft-hearted that they will let you go on without
it, but most have to be propitiated with something,
even a knife. I have even known a brakesman
swap hats when his own was a worse-looking
article. In Texas and New Mexico and Arizona,
it is no uncommon sight to see two or three fellows
riding comfortably on the top of the cars with the
trainmen without anyone objecting, even the officials
at the stations, for the conductor himself gets a

share of the few dollars the tramps are able to afford.

I have often seen the "caboose," or conductor's car, half full of people ; but the conductor pocketed most of the cash. One day two young niggers got on east of Sweetwater, which then, by the way, had the reputation of being one of the most murderous towns in North-west Texas, and the conductor asked them before everybody if they had any money. "If not, you can't ride"; that was his ultimatum.

Boys have the easiest time beating their way, for most conductors are not hard on them, especially if they prepare a yarn that they are going home to see a dying relation, and besides they often have more cheek or "gall" than their grown-up friends. One conductor on the M. K. & T. told me that a boy got on in Missouri once. When he was asked for his ticket, he candidly confessed that he had none. "Then you can't ride," said my friend, and went about his business, thinking the youth would take the hint. But not a bit of it; after the next stopping place, he was still there. "What's this?" said the conductor, "didn't I tell you to get off?" "No," answered the boy simply, "all that you said was that I couldn't ride." "Indeed, well, this time I tell you to get off." He thought that would settle it, and yet after the next station the simple youth was still there. "How's this!" began the conductor, "didn't I tell you to get off?" "Yes,

sir, you did ; but you never said I was to stay off."
The trainman eyed the youth up and down, thinking
he was very soft, or very smart. "Well, bub, that
is so, but now I tell you to get off, and *stay* off."
But next time he was still there. Surely the boy
could have no further excuses. He stared at him
for a while, and all the passengers were laughing.
" Come now, young fellow, what's this mean ?
Didn't I tell you to get off, and stay off ?" The
lad looked up without changing a muscle, and piped
out " Yes, sir, I know you did, but as I stood on
the platform you said ' All aboard,' and so I
thought you had changed your mind !" The
passengers burst into a roar of laughter, in which
the conductor at last joined. " Well, my boy,"
said he, "where do you want to go to ?" " To
Hannibal, sir." " Very well, then, you can ride, I
think you've earned it." Of course I did not learn
all this at once. It had to be painfully knocked
into me. But there was a certain fascination in
travelling without paying I admit.

So seeing nothing else for it, I made up my mind
to act on my friend, the brakesman's, suggestion,
and, as a preparatory step I made a small bundle of
some things I wanted, and packing the rest in my
valise I expressed it down to Santa Fé in New
Mexico. After paying my bill at the boarding-
house I still had seven or eight dollars, which I
carefully stowed away, and that night went down
to the yards with my new friend, who, true to his

promise, hid me away in a car. It was dark and damp, and did not smell very nice, but it was cheap riding and that was what I wanted, so I made up my mind to lump the unpleasantness of my position for the sake of economy.

I was surprised, and not a little disgusted, when daylight came in to make the discovery that the car had last been used to convey hogs, and it had only had a rough clean out since, and as I had been lying on the floor all night, I was in a bit of a mess and had an unpleasant odour hanging about me for some time after. It was soon after daylight that we got to a place called Emporia, and the car that I was in was switched out of the train and left in the yard there. Not being used to this kind of travelling I was pretty glad to break my journey. I waited for some time in the car, not caring to come out, as I did not like anybody to see me, being new to this business. However, after a bit I mustered up courage and made a start, but I saw nobody about, so I soon got out of the yard and took a walk up the main street.

This town was a very quiet little place, and as it happened to be Sunday when I got there it was strikingly dull. There was nothing to be done that day I could see, so not caring to incur more expense than was necessary, I got something to eat at a lunch stand that was in the depôt, and put the day in lounging about the town. Towards evening I began to feel very tired, and this brought to my

mind thoughts of a bed, but I could see that my
little stock of money would not last long if I
indulged in any such luxuries. So as it was now
getting dark I began to look about for a place to
have a sleep. For a long time I could not alight
upon a suitable spot, till at last, as I was walking
along the railway track looking to the right and
left to see if there was anything like a barn or a
haystack that would be likely to give me a bit of
shelter for the night, I passed over a culvert that
ran under the railroad, and, as there did not appear
to be any water in the ditch, I jumped down to
examine it, and to my joy found it quite dry, and
lined with wood; it was about three feet square
and perhaps 25 or 30 feet long. As the wind did
not happen to be blowing right through it on this
occasion, it made on the whole not a bad lodging.
There was a rank growth of grass, which was now
dead and dried like hay as it stood, in the ditch on
either side of the track, so, taking my knife, I soon
had a good lot of it cut, and spreading it on the
bottom of the culvert, with my bundle as a pillow,
I made a much more comfortable bed than I had
had the night before, or many times since for that
matter. I found my lodging so comfortable that I
slept till the sun was well up the next morning.

Pulling one of the slabs down that the culvert
was lined with, I planted my bundle there and
sallied out to see if I could find any work. I
asked everywhere that I thought at all likely, but

it was all the same thing, things were dull, and no work to be had anywhere. I now began to feel rather blue. That evening I got the information from a man I talked with that there was a railroad in course of construction at a place called Council Grove, about 20 miles north of Emporia, and that there was a good chance of getting work. Hearing of nothing else I jumped on the train next morning and went to Council Grove. I had to pay for this journey as there was only one train in the 24 hours, and it went in the daytime. This was another dollar out of my stock, and to use an expression I heard a man make about his own, my pocket-book began to look as if an elephant had stepped on it.

On arriving at Council Grove I found I had to walk seven or eight miles to get to the camp. It being then too late to start that day I was forced to spend more money for a lodging in a house, as it was still winter and a cold snap had set in, making it too severe to sleep out of doors. Next morning I started out in company with another man who was on the same lay as myself, and about noon we arrived at the camp. I inquired for the boss, and on finding him, asked for work; he hired me at once at a dollar and forty cents a day, and informed me that I should have to pay $3 a week for board. He told me I need not go to work that day, but to go down to the camp and have a rest.

The camp consisted of a number of tents pitched in a clump of stunted cotton-wood trees, about half a mile from where the work was going on. There were two big tents that served as dining rooms, and a cooking tent, and three or four for sleeping purposes, besides some private ones belonging to men who had their wives and families with them and boarded themselves. The whole place had a very miserable and squalid appearance which at once gave me a fit of the blues that lasted me for the rest of the day. When night came I found out that there was nothing in the shape of bed-clothes in the camp, excepting the private property of the working men, and, as I had none, I stood a good chance of sleeping cold, and certainly should have done so if a man had not taken pity on me and shared his blanket with me. For this kindness I was very thankful, as the night was bitterly cold and the tent draughty; and although we had a stove there was nothing to burn in it, because the timber round about was private property and none of it could be cut.

In the morning we were all roused out before daylight by somebody beating a kerosine tin, and shouting "hash-pile!" which my bed-fellow informed me was the signal that breakfast was ready, and adding that the first crowd in gets the best show, he kicked the blankets off and jumped up, and I followed his example. No dressing was necessary, as nearly everybody turned in all standing. We made our way to one of the boarding tents, and were fortunate enough to get in with the first crowd.

What the second crowd got I cannot say; what we who were first had was enough to sicken anyone who was not used to it. It consisted of vile greasy fried pork and soda bread just hot out of the oven, and like putty; molasses and coffee like mud. But I was hungry, and was beginning to learn not to be too particular, so I ate some of the horrible stuff and drank a little coffee.

After breakfast was over we all went down to the work, the boss sending me with a gang of men who were working in a " rock cut," as they called it. It was a place where the ground was rather high, and of a rocky nature, and so a shallow cutting had to be made. My work was loading the waggons with the fragments of rock and stuff got out by the blasting gang. I worked here as long as the job lasted, but that was only a week, for the weather began to get so severe that the contractor decided to " shut down " the work till spring, so everybody was paid off. When my board bill and a few things I had had from the store were taken out of my week's wages, I think it was 90 cents I had to take. Considering it had cost me about two dollars to get the job and I had worn out as much in clothes and shoe leather, this could scarcely be considered profitable work. Leaving Council Grove, I went back to Emporia poorer by about a dollar than when I had left it, besides having put in a week of as hard and miserable work as ever I did in my life before or since. The weather, although very cold, was dry, so I took up my quarters in the culvert again; I improved it by stopping up one end with a lot of stones and rubbish, and so made it quite a com- fortable lodging. I stayed about here for three or four days, eating as little as I could, so as to make the money which I still had last as long as possible. However, be as careful as I would, it went little by little until one fine morning I found myself with just one five-cent piece (or a nickel, as they call it in the States) in my pocket, and no prospect of being able to get any more. As far as I could see there was nothing but starvation in front of me if I could not get some kind of employment. I hung on this five-cent all that day, and starved just to get my hand in. Next day it was too much for me, and I went up town in the morning determined to spend the five cents in something to eat.

Now, the momentous question was what to buy; what would be the most substantial and satisfying thing I could get. There was not much choice, but I walked about for at least an hour before I could decide on what would be best, and at last determined to take cheese and crackers. I went into a store where a girl served me, and I believe she suspected what was up with me, for she gave me far more than I have ever had since for five cents. In fact, she gave me so much that with economy it lasted me for three meals, and as I only allowed myself one meal a day, that was three days. After I had eaten up the last scrap of my cheese and crackers I began to feel terribly blue; the idea of begging, or "bumming," as it is popularly called out there, went strongly against my stomach, but that or starvation seemed now the only two things open to me. I stuck out for the whole of that day, but at night as I was going home to my culvert I had to pass a boarding-house that was much frequented by railroad men; as I passed the door the boss came running out, and calling to me asked if I wanted a job. Of course I said I did, so he told me his second cook, or dish washer, had been suddenly taken sick, and he wanted a man temporarily. Of course I jumped at the chance. My wages were to be fifty cents a day and as much grub as I could eat; this last clause in the agreement was what tickled my fancy at that time, and I suggested to the boss that I should like to take a little of it in advance. He readily agreed to this, and said, " Why in thunder, if you were hungry, did you not come and tell me? You could always have had something to eat"; and he added, when I said that I was ashamed to beg, that I was a "darned fool" any way to go hungry when I could get food for the asking.

There was no place for me to sleep on the premises, so the boss used to give me twenty-five cents every night to pay for a bed; this I put in my pocket, and went to my dry culvert instead. So I made seventy-five cents a day instead of only fifty. I was here twelve days altogether, and became quite expert at washing dishes and pots and pans ; in fact, the cook one day told me confidentially that I was a great deal more use to him than the regular man.

When I settled up with the boss here I had $9, and I felt quite rich.

After this I went out in the country and got a job for a few days husking corn, but wishing to go further west, in the hope of getting more work and a better climate, I watched my chance one day and got on a west-bound freight train. However, the brakesman found me, and because I would not give him any money he put me off at the first stop, a place called Haughton. This was only what is called a way station. There was nothing but a section house and a long siding, besides the usual offices attached to a small station. I inquired for work here, but was told to go back about two miles and I should find another section house, where I should most likely be able to get work that would be permanent as long as I wished to stay. So being rather disgusted with my poor success at travelling, I made up my mind to take a job if I could get one, and put off going west till spring.

So I set off back again, and in due course came to the gang. On asking the boss for a job, he said he wanted a man, but the section house had been burned down a few days before, and as he and his

family and all his gang were living in a barn, he
did not know where he could find room for another.
However, on my expressing my willingness to put
up with anything, he said I should stay there that
night anyhow, and he would see what could be
done.

It was well on in the afternoon, and as I had not
had anything to eat all day, I was rather hungry;
the section boss (I forget his name) was a very
good fellow indeed, and no doubt suspecting that
such was the case, sent me up to the barn where
he was camping and told me to ask the old woman
for something to eat. I went up and found the
place much more comfortable than I had expected
it would be. The old woman was about twenty-six
or seven I should say, and rather pretty, but when I
communicated my business to her, she informed me
she was too old to be had by a tale of that kind,
but I could have something to eat if I would chop
some firewood for her. I said nothing, but took
the axe she gave me and went to the wood pile. I
had only chopped two or three pieces when she came
to the door and said " all right, drop that axe, and
come inside and sit down; I only wanted to see if
you would work, I don't believe in feeding
professional bums."

As soon as she got me inside the house she
assailed me with a shower of questions and never
stopped till she had asked and got an answer to
every question she could think of.

It was now close on dark, and she set about fixing the table for the gang to have supper. This occupation kept her tongue quiet a bit, and presently the men came in and we all sat down to the best meal I had had for a long while; for, with all her faults, and they were many, the boss's wife was a good cook.

CHAPTER IV.

JOINT AHEAD AND CENTRE BACK.

AFTER we had eaten our supper, which was as I have
said the best I had had for a considerable time, the
question of sleeping accommodation came up, and
I was shown into the hay loft of the barn which
was the sleeping apartment of the whole gang. We
were altogether 10 in number. There was a good
pile of soft hay at one end, and by pulling this down
and spreading the blankets that the boss lent me on
it, I very soon made a much more comfortable bed
than I had slept on for some time. It certainly
was better than the culvert though not so private.
I was glad to have some place to sleep and work at,
for the winter in this country was beginning to get
very severe. Kansas, though it seems to be a good
way to the south, is rather high up, and knocking
about and sleeping in the open air begins at this
time of the year to be not only uncomfortable, but
even dangerous.

It is true the wages for this job were not very
large. They were only a dollar and ten cents a
day, and out of this I had to pay three dollars a
week for board. But I was glad then to get any-

thing which promised to be permanent. I must put the winter in somehow, and though I did not like pick and shovel work, 1 would rather do that than nothing, when nothing meant going without food and sleeping anywhere with a good chance of being frozen to death while doing it; and fortunately those who worked with me were pretty good fellows.

As soon as breakfast was over in the morning we went out to work. Section work is track repairing ; every line in the United States is divided into divisions of various lengths, but about 150 to 200 miles is the general length of them. Each division is under the supervision of a man who is called a division road master. Every division is again subdivided into sections varying in length from three or four miles up to as much as 10 miles according as the track is easy or difficult to keep in order. The sections are each presided over by a section boss, who has eight or ten labourers under him. The section boss is held responsible for the condition of his own section. I was now in the position of a railroad labourer, and as the boss was a very good fellow he looked over my shortcomings and helped me to learn my work. The work, as I said before, consists in keeping the track in order. In wet weather, when the road-bed is not well ballasted, the joints of the rails are very liable to sink out of the level, and the track to get out of line, and section work consists chiefly in remedying

these defects, which are technically called low joints
and high centres. As the boss gives his orders to
his men, the expressions "joint ahead and centre
back" are continually in his mouth to indicate to
the men the places he wishes raised; these words
are used so much that they have passed into a kind
of a by-word, and there is a song in which the refrain
is—

> "Joint ahead and centre back
> And Johnny go oil the car."

Though the work was hard and dirty I did not find
my position so bad as one might imagine. My
greatest trouble here was the children. The boss
had married a woman who had been divorced, and
besides his own children he had got a whole host of
infernal young imps that belonged to his wife's
former husband. These little beasts tried all they
could to make things as uncomfortable as possible.
I never fully realised till this time how really
exasperating badly brought up children could be.
One Sunday, shortly after my arrival here, I heard
the "Missis'," as we all called her, send one of the
younger children out to tell her eldest boy to come
to the house, as she wanted him. The message he
sent back was "You tell the old woman if she wants
me just to keep on wanting, there is a sight better
people than her that has had to die wanting." On
receiving this message she went to the door and
shouted out "All right, my buck, when I get a holt
of you, I'll knock the stuffing clean out of you."

This was the kind of thing that was going on all the time when any of them were awake.

I had only secured myself a place to stay just in time, for the weather began to get worse and worse every day. Snow began to fall, and the thermometer was often down to zero, and sometimes below.

Every morning we used to go out on the track and do what was possible to be done, which, now the frosts had fairly set in, was not much. However, we tinkered along as best we could, as a day lost meant a day's pay lost and the board bill to be paid just the same. Sometimes, however, the weather was so severe that it was quite impossible to do anything. On these occasions we stayed at home and sat round the fire, one man being sent out to walk over the track and see if there were any broken rails. For this he received his day's pay just the same as if he had been at work with the pick and shovel. All the rails being steel on this line, it was necessary to keep a sharp look-out on them as they will fly just like glass in frosty weather. Several bad railway accidents have happened from this cause. In the majority of cases the snap is so clean that a green hand would most likely pass it by without noticing it at all, for it looks hardly more noticeable than a hair laid across the rail.

About three weeks after I came to work at this place we were whistled up in the middle of the night by the east-bound mail. They had passed over a broken rail which, to use the popular expression, had nearly " ditched the train." The broken rail was about three miles west of the section house and at the top of a steep grade. Of course we had to turn out at once to repair the damage. The first thing was to go down to the tool-house and put what is called a hand-car on the line and go about half a mile east, to get a new rail from a place where a number of them was kept for such occasions as the present. After getting the rail we came back to the tool-house, and taking what tools were necessary for the job, we started to the broken rail. Considering the thermometer was 10° below zero and a blinding snowstorm was beating in our face, this was a job of no small magnitude. Shoving the car loaded with a steel rail and a lot of tools up a steep grade under such conditions as I have described is anything but child's play.

When we got to work we had to place red lamps each side of us to warn anything that might be coming along that the line was not safe, and it took one man all he could do running from one lamp to another and brushing the snow off them so as to allow the light to be seen, even at a very short distance. From the time we left the section house till we got back was about four hours, but during that time I had suffered as much acute agony from the bitter cold and the touching of frozen iron as some more fortunate people are called on to go through in a lifetime. When we got up to the house we were glad to find that the "Missis" was up and had made a big pot of hot coffee for us. I was more thankful for a cup of that coffee than I should have been for a cupful of twenty dollar gold pieces. We received a day's pay for this job, that being the rule when men are called out at night, even if the job does not last more than half an hour. And in my opinion that four hours' work was worth a month's pay or as much more as a rich man would give to be let off taking his share in it.

As a general rule there was much sameness about this section' work. It was pick and shovel and tamping bar day in and day out. It was only the conditions of frost and snow under which it often had to be done that made it a little less monotonous if more painful. One day, when we had decided that the weather was altogether too bad to go out to work, as the thermometer was down 15° below zero and a piercing north-easterly wind blowing, carrying the frozen snow along in clouds, we were sitting round the stove,which we had been carefully nursing till we had it red hot all over and half-way up the pipe; and as we were congratulating ourselves on the warmth, a west-bound coal train pulled up opposite the section house and set his whistle going for all he was worth. Of course we had to go and see what it was the trainmen wanted.

The conductor met the boss as he was going down to the track, and told him that about half-way between our place and Emporia yards they had run over a cow. How the perverse beast happened to be on the track beat us all to find out, as cattle at this time of the year are in barns or under shelters that are built especially for the purpose. She had thrown a car off in the middle of the train. The rest of the train had kept the track all right, and towing this one car along for a distance of about a quarter of a mile, had raked all the spikes out of the sleepers (or ties, as they are called in the States), and broken the heads off the fish-plate bolts for the whole of that distance. This damage meant a stoppage in all traffic till it was repaired. We all had to muffle up and start out at once. I do not think that any of the men who were with me will ever forget that day. Although we of course wore the most serviceable mittens that could be got, the frozen iron and steel that we had to be continually handling occasioned me, at least, the most exquisite pain. I felt as if my hands had been severely burnt and then my finger ends been jambed in a door. There was no such thing as shirking at this job, for we were all too anxious to get it over. However, work as hard as we would, it took us nearly all day.

. This job was really worse than putting in the broken rail, as it lasted much longer and the weather was much colder. The only advantage

we had was the daylight. When we returned to
the section house after finishing, we made the
discovery that two of the gang had got their feet
frozen. This was a serious matter and had to be
attended to at once; the regulation specific was
applied in both cases, *i.e.*, rubbing with snow. One
of these men was an Irishman, and to do him
justice he stood the pain of recovery like a brick,
but the other one, who was an Alabama man, roared
like a bull and nearly brought the rafters down. I
was not surprised at it, as, although I was not
actually frozen, the pain I experienced when I
began to get warm was such as to make it a very
difficult matter for me not to follow his example
and yell.

However, I contented myself with indulging in a
considerable amount of profanity in chorus with
the gang, chiefly directed against the luckless cow
who had been the unconscious cause of all the
trouble.

This day's work was about the worst I had while
I was on this section. After this the weather
seemed to moderate; there was not so much hard
frost for the rest of the winter, and work was much
less uncomfortable than it had been.

There was one man in the gang, by name Hiram
Ramp, quite a young fellow, but about six feet tall,
and broad in proportion. What we should have
done without him I really do not know, as he was

the life of the whole gang. But on one occasion he came very near being the death of us all by way of a change.

It occurred thus.—We were working one day at the top of Haughton grade or incline, which was about two and a half or three miles long, and terminated in a sharp curve where a small trestle bridge crosses Plum Creek. It was evening, and our work being done for that day, we put the hand car on the line, and loading our tools on, we started for home, the boss standing by the brake to prevent the car from gaining too much way. Now it must surely have been the very devil of mischief who put it into Mr. Hiram's head to pick up the oil can and pour a stream of oil on the brake-wheel. No one saw him do it, but the effect became at once apparent by the increased velocity with which the car shot down the grade, and the inability of the boss to use the brake effectively.

Things now looked grave, for if we reached the bottom of the grade going at the rate we should have attained when we got there, it was patent to every one of us that the car must leave the track, which meant that we should all be flung into the dry bed of Plum Creek and dashed to pieces. However, this was not to be, for when we were about three-quarters of the way down, going, I should say, at least 35 or 40 miles an hour, we passed a "low joint" or a "high centre," which-ever the inequality in the track might be; the car left the track with a bound, and shooting us up in the air, amongst a shower of crowbars, pickaxes, shovels, and other tools, landed us all in the ditch, which fortunately was full of snow, for that was the only thing that saved us. Strange to say, no one was seriously hurt; there were plenty of bruises and scratches, but nothing of a serious nature. The car was lying bottom up, and was most completely wrecked ; if anyone had happened to fall under it he must have been smashed to pieces.

On examining the remains of the car the boss found out what was up, and, knowing Hiram's weakness for larking, he taxed him with it. He owned it at once, and said he did it for a lark. " And one," said the boss, " which has nearly cost us all our lives. I'll give you your time when we get to the house, and you can go and lark somewhere else."

He did get the sack, but was taken on again shortly afterwards ; but I think he got too much of a scare to try that trick again. At any rate, he was not likely to play it on me, for spring was now pretty near, and I began to think of going on towards New Mexico.

After I had been at work at this Haughton section for a short time, I had sent down to Santa Fé, and had my baggage returned to me, and I now had more on hand than it was convenient to carry ; so, not caring to be bothered, I turned as much as I could into money.

I also swapped my rifle to a farmer that lived near, getting a Smith and Wesson revolver and $5 in cash for it. They only pay every month on the sections, and for the time men have put in since the last pay day they have to take what is called a time check, which is only negotiable at the head-quarters of the road; or if it is too much trouble to go up to head-quarters, the man who is leaving will sell it to the boss for what he will give, which is generally about half what it is worth. As I thought it would now be good weather down south, I determined to start off at once. I took a time check, as I was going up to Topeka anyway.

Having to pay board, and losing so much time on account of bad weather, my money did not foot up a great amount. I think $12 was about all I could muster, including what I had on my time check. This was certainly not a great deal to take after about 4½ months of the kind of work I had been at on this section. But it had to do.

CHAPTER V.

OFF BREAKS!

I NOW had all my possessions about me, and they consisted of little else than the clothes I stood upright in. I tramped from the section house into Emporia, where I managed to jump a freight the same night and got right up to Topeka without any trouble. On arriving at Topeka I went to the office and cashed my check, which was for four dollars. I then put up at the house I had been staying at before and began to make inquiries as to the best means of obtaining a " labour pass " down to some part of New Mexico. There happened to be a man staying at the same house, who also wanted to go down there, and as he was a native of the country and knew all the wrinkles, I was very fortunate to fall in with him. He introduced me to a man named Jerome Bricker, who was getting a gang of men together to go down to a place called San Marcial in New Mexico. The work was to be fencing the railroad, and the pay $1 60 c. a day, $3 a week to be paid for board.

He engaged me at once, but as it would be a week before he was ready to start I had all that time on my hands.

I at once went down to the boarding-house and paid a week's board which cost me $5 out of my little stock. I then bought a blanket, after paying for which I was very nearly " busted " again; but having my immediate wants supplied and having secured a job that would last all the summer if I wanted to stay, I cared little about my financial position being rather a bad one.

Having nothing to do but loaf round, I spent all my time wandering about the town and saw at times some peculiarly American sights.

It being the spring of the year and the frosts having broken up, Topeka was one vast mud-hole. The town authorities had a kind of a machine like a snow plough on a small scale, but having certain modifications to suit it to the different kind of work it had to perform. With this they were ploughing the mud off the street car track. There were at least 16 mules hitched to this arrangement and they often got stuck and could not budge a foot. This was in the main street of the town; Kansas Avenue I believe was the name of it. Some of the smaller streets were mere rivers of liquid mud.

During my stay here I witnessed a sight no doubt common enough to the natives, but I had never seen anything like it before. This was what is called an " ice gorge." The Caw or " Kansas

River," as it is sometimes called, was in flood, and whirling down in its turbid stream vast quantities of ice together with all sorts of débris known in this country by the name of "flood trash." Some of the sheets of ice were apparently as much as several hundred superficial feet in extent, and from three to four feet in thickness. These huge blocks and slabs of ice were crushing and grinding one over the other, and sometimes shooting up vertically to a height of 15 or 20 feet above the level of the rest and then falling over with a dull crushing sound that gave one a better idea than anything else could of their immense weight.

The "gorge" or "jamb" was occasioned by some of these large pieces of ice getting piled in such a manner across the river as to form a sort of barrier or dam which backed the water up to a height of several feet, even above its flood level; but of course the weight of the backed up water was such that nothing could resist it long. Accordingly in about two hours, during which time an immense quantity of ice had accumulated, the "gorge" broke, and the crushing and grinding of the ice as one block leaped over the other and fell with fearful force on the rest, together with the rushing and roaring of the liberated torrent, made a sight which has to be seen to be properly appreciated. Of course the whole volume of the river was not stopped or the jamb could not have stood it five minutes.

I saw nothing more of great interest while I was
here, and to fill up time was hard put to it loafing
and holding the sidewalk down as they say there.
But in due course the day came round when we
were to make a start for New Mexico and our work.
It was night when our crowd left Topeka from the
Atchison, Topeka, and Santa Fé railroad depôt;
and for this I was not very sorry, as the whole State
of Kansas is pretty flat and uninteresting. That
night we got over a good deal of ground although
the travelling was pretty slow, for the train has to
climb all the way from Topeka to the mountains.
Though Kansas is flat it is not horizontal, but
one long ascent from east to west. Towards the
middle of the next day, when a bend in the track
enabled us to look west, we could just see far to
the north and south the blue line of the Rocky
Mountains. At times the condition of the atmo-
sphere would blear them out altogether, and at
others they were as sharply defined as the teeth
of a saw, sometimes of a pale misty blue and again
of a deep purple which changed to a sombre grey
that looked almost black. They continually varied
in colour, but after hours of travel they still
appeared the same distance off until nightfall hid
them from view.

The next morning we were in the "foot hills"
climbing up steep grades with a slowness which
would have been monotonous and irritating but
for the beauty of the scenery. We wound along the

sides of precipitous mountains and crossed great gulches on what appeared most slight and airy structures, but which wore I suppose quite serviceable trestle bridges. Then we passed through deep cuttings with here and there gaps through which could be seen the mountains rising peak beyond peak and terrace beyond terrace. Sometimes these peaks seemed to fade slowly into the deep blue of the sky, and then they again appeared to once more bury themselves in a low hanging cloud. This was blown aside after awhile to give us a glimpse of some snow-covered heights that looked like phantoms and made me rub my eyes to see if I had not made a mistake in thinking they were mountains at all.

It was in the afternoon of this day that we passed through the Raton pass and tunnel. The grades here are so heavy that special locomotives are kept on this division to get the trains over the pass. On leaving Trinidad, which is the last division terminus before getting to the Raton mountains, they put a second large engine on behind the train, and with this additional help it crawls up the pass at about a good walking pace. In fact there were some horses on the track, and they would pay no attention to the whistle, so the brakesman and conductor got off, and running ahead of the train pelted them out of the way, and then got on again. Going through the cutting which brings down the approach to the tunnel, there are large veins of coal in places two or three feet thick, to be seen running through the red earth across which the cutting is made. After leaving the Raton Pass we crossed the Glorietta mountains and descended into the Rio Grande bottom, as it is called here, but is better described as the valley of the Rio Grande, which bisects the territory of New Mexico from north to south. It is a broad fertile valley all under cultivation, with a system of irrigation, the water for which is supplied from the Rio Grande, and carried all over the plain by innumerable irrigating ditches or *xequias*. This system of ditches or xequias is kept in order by the agricultural part of the population, who turn out at certain times of the year and, under the guidance of bosses selected for their knowledge and experience of the work, make what repairs or alterations are necessary.

The population consists chiefly of Mexicans and Pueblo Indians, and mixtures of the two. These Pueblo Indians, very harmless and industrious, are nearly related to the Zuni, or, as most people call them about here, the Montezuma Indians.

The Pueblos, or small walled towns that are scattered over this valley, are extremely picturesque, and every one of them that I saw had a small church built of adobes or bricks baked in the sun. These bricks, of which all the native houses are built in this part of the country, although they are spelt " adobes," I always heard them spoken of as " dobies."

On the evening of the day we passed the Raton mountains we arrived at San Marcial, and as the boarding cars had to be fitted up, the cooking appliances put in order, &c., we were sent to an hotel, or what they chose to call one, till these arrangements were completed, which was not till the evening of the following day.

I was surprised and not very pleased to find out that the small-pox was making fearful havoc with the country. Whole villages were depopulated in some parts of the surrounding district.

The second day after our arrival the railroad doctor came round and vaccinated the whole gang, all but two men, who, refusing to submit to the operation, were at once discharged. All houses that had an inmate sick with the small-pox were draped with strips of yellow and black calico : I do not know whether they were obliged to do it, or whether it was merely a custom of the country. At San Marcial there were very few houses that were not decorated in this manner.

But, small-pox or not, we had to get to work, and as there was plenty of material on the spot all ready for us we made a start at once.

The job at which I was put first was digging post holes, and as the ground was pretty hard in places, I found it rather a tough job; but in a day or two I got used to the work, and as the weather was then mild without being hot, I could do quite as much as was expected of me. But soon the heat began to get greater and greater every day, until I was as much too hot as I had been too cold up in Kansas. However, I could put up with that, and would have been able to enjoy myself very well if it had not been for the dust and sand storms which were now beginning to be very bad indeed.

Although we started work at San Marcial, we only did a little bit there, and then shifted to a place further north called Bernalillo, which was our head-quarters for some time. The first Sunday we were here, I, in company with some others of the gang, made a trip up Sandia or the Melon mountain. Though the sun was scorching in the valley, after about two hours' climbing we began to come to snow and ice in the crevices of the rocks, which had not melted since the winter before, and at last it began to get so cold that I concluded I had gone far enough.

As we were going back we struck the railroad track some two miles south of where we were working. Walking along the track we overtook an old Indian (a very fine-looking man he was, too), who informed us in broken English that he was a chief, and that his name was Sandia, the same as the mountain we had just come from. He carried a fine silver-headed Malacca cane on which was engraved " Presented to Sandia by President Lincoln," also a date which I forget. The old fellow seemed immensely proud of it, and carried it stuck through his belt as a Japanese wears a sword.

I shall always remember the time I spent here, as I got an attack of ophthalmia that nearly drove me mad. I have suffered pain in various ways, but nothing I ever experienced drove me so nearly mad as this. The agony was terrible; for nights and days I never slept, but lay on my back with wet tea leaves bandaged on my eyes. This was the only thing that gave me any relief. I was attended by a doctor from Bernalillo, and one day when I was at the worst I told him that if he could not do something to relieve the pain I would blow my brains out, and I meant it too. The cook heard what I said, and was so convinced I was in earnest that she came in and took my revolver away from the head of my bunk. However, that afternoon the doctor came back and injected either morphia or cocaine into one of my arms, which operation he repeated several times during the next two or three days. This gave me some rest, and from this time I began to get better, but it was more than two weeks before I could go to work again, and then I had to wear blue glasses. For a long time my eyes were very weak, and I saw everything double. Our work here was enlivened by frequent rows with the Mexicans through whose land the railroad passed. These people declared that the railroad company had no right to fence in their land without giving them some compensation; and I think they had a real grievance, for a piece of land twenty yards wide, and sometimes as much as half a mile long, was a considerable slice off a small farm.

However, of course we could not help the action of the company, but it was sometimes very hard to make these ignorant peasants understand this. I did not mind the men so much, although some of them were very truculent-looking savages, who, if appearances were anything to judge by, were fit for anything desperate. These jokers, when they saw that they had irritated us to the verge of retaliation, would clear out and leave us alone. But the women were not to be got rid of so easily. There was one place on the job that did not get fenced for a long time just on account of three women— a mother and two daughters. These were the greatest viragoes I ever saw. The first attempt we made to get the fence up they turned out and ordered us off, and as we did not go they pelted us with stones, and as quick as a peg was driven in to mark the position of a post hole one of them would run up and pull it out. One day they were away to town or somewhere, so we got all the post holes sunk; but next morning, when we came on the scene, we found that they had filled them all up again during the night. The boss then turned all the gang on to the job and finished it in one day, and got the wire stretched; after this they left it alone. Passing down this way some five or six months after I noticed that they had demolished the whole business, not leaving a single post standing on their land.

I was now getting very tired of this work, which became monotonous after the Mexicans came to the conclusion that they had better leave us alone. So being offered a job to go out to the Moore and Casey Ranch on the Rio d'Acoma, I gave Bricker notice and left; but when I *had* left it appeared that the man who had hired me had no authority from Messrs. Moore and Casey to do anything of the kind, as they had all the help they wanted. So I was once more adrift with next to nothing in my pocket, and this time in a wilder country than ever.

However, there was no help for it. I have no doubt that Bricker would have taken me back again if I had asked him, but I would not. We were then at a place called Albuquerque, which is the largest town in the State of New Mexico. It is made up of the old and new towns, the latter of which is the American quarter, consisting of some stores, hotels, &c., near the railroad depôt, while the former part is built of adobe, and is inhabited by Mexicans and half-bred Indians. That the town is pretty advanced as far as modern civilisation goes out in the West is evident from the fact that they were introducing the telephone into it. I was fortunate to get a job at this work, and being a sailor the climbing up the posts to fix the wires came very easy to me. I gave such satisfaction to the boss that he said, when I left after about ten days, " If you are ever round this way again and want a job, come to me, for you have picked up the working of this thing a deal quicker than any man I ever had."

However, I did not think it likely I should ever trouble him for employment again. The town was as dull as the work, and climbing posts with climbing irons on my feet all day long, and with the bight of a wire in one's hands, was not particularly attractive to me. Besides, I was terribly restless, and never content unless I was going somewhere or other. Men were always talking together, saying this or the other is a good place to go to; and now most spoke of Colorado. So there I at last determined to go.

When I had settled my board bill and bought a new pair of boots I had just 50 cents left, and with this small sum I struck out for the mountains. Jumping an east bound freight at Albuquerque, I managed to hold it down or keep on it till I got to a place called Alameda, where I was spotted by an avaricious " breaky," and because I would not " put up " was put off. Knowing that there would not be another train through that night, and not wishing to be left there till the next day, I got off, walked away, and coming back on the other side of the train, I sneaked on to the cow-catcher, where, under the glare of the head lights, I was secure from observation. In this manner I got up to Wallace, which was as far as I wanted to go on

this line. Although I was down enough on brakesmen this journey, and hated some of them badly
enough to commit manslaughter, yet I own to
thinking all the money they could rake up would
not compensate them properly for their work; for
the occupation of a brakesman on a freight train is
about one of the hardest, and certainly most
dangerous, jobs which I know. I have heard people
talking of the danger of a seafaring life and other
occupations in connexion with the sea. But no
business I ever saw is, to my way of thinking, so
hazardous as that of a brakesman. It is no doubt
made a great deal worse than it need be by the
carelessness, not only of the brakesmen themselves,
but of engine drivers and switchmen, and others
who work with them; but whoever it is that makes
the blunder, the poor devil of a brakesman is in the
place of danger, and as a general thing gets the
benefit of it. The fact that no insurance company
will insure a brakesman's life speaks volumes for the
dangerous nature of the calling. When I was at
Emporia, in Kansas, there was a young brakesman
had his right arm cut off just above the elbow by
the carelessness or ignorance of the man who was
driving the yard engine. The brakesman was
standing by to couple the cars that the yard engine
was backing down on to the rest of the train; the
driver sent them down with such force as to
telescope the two cars, the brakesman saw what was
going to happen and made a jump out, but though

he escaped with his life, he lost his arm. I heard that the company gave him something, but what it was I do not know—little enough for the loss of an arm, no doubt, whatever it was.

Though dangerous enough in itself a brakesman's job is rendered doubly bad by circumstances of weather. For instance, on a bitterly cold night in winter with a thermometer down to 15 or 20 degrees below zero and a gale of wind blowing, the train comes to a steep grade, the engineer whistles for brakes. The brakesman then has to go out and walk perhaps half the length of a long train on a board about 18 inches wide, which is covered with snow and ice, and so slippery as to make it a most difficult thing for him to keep his feet. Add to this that the train is in most cases oscillating and jumping about on a rough track; and it will be at once apparent that the man is in a most perilous position, for a fall in such a case means certain death by being cut to pieces under the train. All the brake handles are of iron, and it is in frosty weather agony to touch them even with heavy gloves on. Frequently the brakesmen are mere boys of 16 or 17 and upwards who have run away from home, this profession standing in the States in much the same position as the sea does in England as employment for runaways. Many of them are frost-bitten every winter, and it is almost impossible to pick up a paper without reading of one or more cases of frightful accidents to some of the poor fellows. The danger of the calling seems to have a sort of charm for the youngsters, for there is never any lack of men to fill any job of the kind that becomes vacant, even if the remains of the man that last occupied it have just been gathered up in a wheelbarrow.

CHAPTER VI.

An Up Grade.

WALLACE was a division terminus, with a round house and machine shops. However, there was nothing of a town there, and I had to expend my last half dollar to get something to eat, for that was the regulation price of a meal, and there was no store to buy anything at at a cheaper rate.

There was an old trail crossing the mountains from this place to Santa Fé, and as that city lay in my way I determined to go there. The road was bad, as it had not been used a great deal since the railroad was opened, nor indeed, as far as I could judge, had it ever been, as it was for most of the way merely a bridle path. The track, such as it was, disappeared entirely in places, but there was no danger of missing the way, as there was only the one pass through the mountains, and it was impossible to mistake it. What the distance really was I do not know, as everybody I ever asked about it either did not know or stated it variously. The weather was fine, and the mountain air cool and bracing; so I might have enjoyed my tramp fairly well if it had not been for the new boots I had bought in Albuquerque, which now began to hurt my feet dreadfully. The path was broken, and strewn with sharp fragments of rock, which made it quite impossible to walk without boots, or I would have taken them off. After travelling I should think four or five miles, the road suddenly topped a ridge, and then dipped down through a rugged gully into a small sandy plain nearly circular in form, and walled all round by precipitous hills. It was, by a rough guess, about a mile across. I was a bit in doubt as to which way to take, but seeing a gully nearly on the opposite side I concluded that must be the way, and accordingly steered for it. The sand being perfectly smooth and hard here, I pulled my boots off, and so walked a little easier, but not much, for the boots had done their work well, and my feet were already skinned in several places.

As I approached the gully I just mentioned, I could see a large stream of water coming down it, foaming in miniature cascades over the rocks and boulders in its course. This rather surprised me, as from the brow of the ridge I had just left I could see all over the valley, but I did not notice a stream of any kind in any part of it. The mystery was explained, however, when I got a bit further along; for although there was a considerable volume of water in the stream, it no sooner left its rocky bed and struck the sandy plain than it disappeared entirely, leaving only a damp smudge on the sand about 100 yards across, reminding me. in a small way, of what I had heard of the Sink of the Humboldt River. As the rocky road commenced again at this point I washed my feet and put on my boots. They now hurt me a great deal more than before, and every step I took was painful; but there was nothing for it but to push on, as the nearest inhabited place was Santa Fé, or to go back again to Wallace. Going back was never much in my line. So, groaning and cursing my fate, I stumbled and hobbled along all the rest of the day, until late in the evening, after the sun was down, I came out on a part of the road where I could see the city of Santa Fé some two or three miles distant.

The sight was a very welcome one to me, for although I had no money, and not the remotest idea of where I was going to earn any, still it was comforting to be near some human beings. It is true I still had my revolver, on which I could have raised some money, but that would only be as a last resource. I was utterly fagged out, not by the walk, which of itself would have been nothing, but by the pain of my feet, which were quite raw and bleeding in several places, and had been so for hours; and, besides, I was weak with hunger, having eaten nothing all day.

Not caring to go any further that night I selected a spot as sheltered as I could find, and, wrapping myself in my blanket, I lay down on the ground, and in spite of hunger and pain I soon went to sleep. I had been asleep some time when I was awakened by the howling of the coyotes. Several of these sneaking beasts were prowling round, some of them being nearly within arm's length of me when I awoke, but when I started up and shouted at them they scampered off. It was a beautifully clear night, without a breath of wind stirring, and a full moon high in the heavens made it almost as light as day. The dark shadows cast by the cactus bushes and clumps of piñon, amongst which every once in a while could be seen a sneaking coyote trailing his long bushy tail in the sand, gave the landscape quite an eerie appearance. Having driven these unwelcome intruders away I rested undisturbed till the sun awakened me in the morning.

I now had to make a start for the city. Getting up, I put on my boots, but the pain was most unbearable. During the night the wounds had partially healed, but bringing them again into contact with the hard leather of my boots rubbed off the partially-formed new skin, and occasioned me the most exquisite agony. After two or three attempts and some excusable profanity, I at last started. After going some little distance, I came to a coral, where some Mexican teamsters were feeding their bullocks with cactus boughs, from which they were burning the prickles on a large fire they had there for the purpose. The cattle were evidently quite used to this rough kind of fodder, and ate it eagerly; whether they ever got anything else I could not say, but they appeared to be strong and well-fed beasts. It was about eight o'clock in the morning when I arrived in Santa Fé, and as I had had nothing to eat since the previous morning, the first thing that struck me was to look for some breakfast. With this idea in my mind, I entered the town, and began to look about to see if there was anything in the shape of work going on, but could see nothing; in fact, the place seemed to be asleep. Two-thirds of the population, as far as I could judge, consisted of Mexicans, and the only industry that appeared to be going ahead was carrying loads of firewood packed on the back of a small kind of ass, called here " burro." The streets were crowded with these animals, whose load in some cases was nearly as big as the beast which was carrying it. I was told that in the mountains where the wood is cut, that the " burros " are made to lie down, their load being then placed on their back. One man then takes hold by their nose, and another the tail, and they are hoisted on to their feet. If on any occasion they happen to fall, the same operation has to be repeated. They are, no doubt, hardy animals, and carry a very large load for their size.

Seeing no chance of getting any work of an ordinary kind, I went up to a house where I saw a large stack of unchopped firewood, and knocking at the door, I asked to be allowed to chop some for my breakfast. The boss said, " Well, I keep a man on monthly wages to do that kind of work, but you may go ahead and chop some, and I will give you something to eat." I accordingly took the axe and went to work. I had not been at it more than 10 minutes or so, when the boss went out. As soon as he was away a fine strapping young negress came out of the house, and looking at me, she exclaimed, " Lord sakes! the poor boy looks as if he was dying. Put that axe right down, and come in and have something to eat." It may be imagined that I was not slow to do as she bade me. She filled me a large basin of water, and giving me a towel, told me to wash my face and hands. I think this wash did quite as much to restore me as the good breakfast which I afterwards got. While I was discussing this meal a very pretty and lady-like woman came into the kitchen (she was the boss's wife), and put me through a series of questions as to my nationality, my paternity, religion, and business out in that part of the world, winding up her interrogations by asking me if I was not very glad to have got away from the power of Queen Victoria. She seemed to be incredulous when I informed her that our Queen was not the merciless and powerful tyrant she seemed to suppose, and that, with some exceptions, the English people did not at all dislike her.

After finishing my breakfast I returned to my job at the wood pile, at which I continued till the boss came home to dinner. He then told me to knock off, and he would take me down to his store in the city, where he had a pile of wood he wished chopped up. After dinner, which I had at this house, I went with my new employer down to his store, where I worked for the rest of the day. After finishing at night, he gave me my supper and a dollar for the work I had done, and showing me a boarding-house, where, he said, I could get a bed for 50 cents, he told me to come to the store at seven o'clock next morning, and he would give me work for a day or two. He said I was not to buy any breakfast in the morning, as I could have some at the store.

Being now possessed of a dollar, and having eaten three good meals in one day, I was pretty spry, in spite of my sore feet, which still gave me a good deal of pain. I did not like the idea of squandering half of my newly-acquired wealth on such a luxury as a bed, but not being able to find any suitable camping-place out of doors, I finally decided to invest a quarter in one. I selected a place, which certainly was a low-down looking shanty enough, but was the only place where I could stay for so small a sum as 25 cents. This house, I afterwards found out, was about the rowdiest shop in the town; indeed I had proof enough of it that night, for I had not been turned

in long, when a man, who went by the name of
Cheyenne Charlie, opened the ball by committing
an assault on the proprietor of the house, who
rejoiced in the name of Pistol Johnny, which he
had acquired by his proficiency in the use of that
weapon, and his readiness to use it on the least
provocation. On the present occasion his wife
prevented bloodshed by concealing his revolvers;
if she had not done so, there would in all
probability have been at least one funeral the next
day. After Cheyenne Charley had been ejected
from the premises, our friend Pistol Johnny turned
himself loose on his wife (who, by the way, was the
ugliest woman I ever saw) for hiding his weapons.
After soothing his ruffled feelings by abusing her
in the vilest terms the English language could
supply for the occasion, he armed himself with
a double-barrelled shot-gun, and sallied out in
pursuit of his enemy; but the city marshal having
by this time heard of the row, he was arrested and
locked up before he had got the length of a block.
His wife went up to the city hall, or wherever it
was that he was locked up, and, on his promising
to behave himself, he was allowed out on bail. For
this good office his poor wife received a hiding,
after which she relieved the monotony of things by
keeping up a lugubrious howl for the rest of the
night, while her amiable husband drank himself
into a state of imbecility, in which condition he
went to sleep under the table.

When I went to the store in the morning, I was put to various odd jobs about the place, shifting packages and opening them, and stowing away the various contents in their several places and pigeon holes. At this kind of work I was kept for the remainder of the time I was here, which was altogether five days. On the evening of the fifth day the boss called me and said he would not require me any more as he had no further work for me to do. Not having spent anything but a quarter a night for my bed at Pistol Johnny's, I had three dollars and seventy-five cents saved, and felt quite a small capitalist on the strength of it.

As I wished to get into Colorado, my road lay north. So striking the trail next morning I started for Española, which was the first town, or rather village, for it was nothing more, that lay in my road. Knowing that I should not be able to make the whole distance, which was 26 miles, in one day, I laid out half a dollar in some cheese and bread. I may as well explain here that the distance between Santa Fé and Española is not covered by a railway line because there is some clause in the charter of either the Denver and Rio Grande, or the Atchison, Topeka, and Santa Fé railroads, which forbids the junction of those two roads for a period of years; it may be joined now but was not at the time I am writing about.

I made about half the distance (13 miles) on this day, determining not to overdo the thing, as my feet were not yet quite well, after the skinning they had got coming over the trail from Wallace. I camped that night in a dry gully, and the coyotes howled dismally, and kept me awake for some time, as they had done in the Santa Fé trail.

I was up as soon as the sun in the morning, and after a feed of bread and cheese and a drink of water, some of which I found in a crevice of the rocks, I started again, and this day completed my journey early in the afternoon. When I arrived at Española I made inquiries about trains, though not with any intention of paying my fare, as that was not possible, and found that there were only two a week running on this line, which is a branch of the Denver and Rio Grande, and joins the main line at a place called Anginita. The distance from Española to this place is 92 miles, the first 50 to the north being all up hill and very fatiguing. I walked the whole distance, and it took me just five days. I renewed my stock of provender at a place called Tres Piedres, where there is a way station, and the depôt agent keeps a small store. I had made inquiries in Española as to the water, and was told that it was scarce and at long intervals, so I supplied myself with an old canteen which I bought from a Mexican shepherd for 15 cents. I found it a most useful possession; in fact I should have been in a hard corner without it, as for the last two days' journey there was absolutely no water to be found along my road. Though I tried for work at every section house, I could obtain none ; but I heard most encouraging accounts of work in saw mills and at the mines further north.

When I arrived in Anginita, I was at an altitude of about 7,000 feet above sea level ; the weather was very cold at nights, for it was early summer as yet, and the summers are always behind in the mountains. There were several sharp frosts, although the month was June.

This being the case, I was anxious to obtain some employment, so that I should have some place to stay in, for it was too cold to sleep out with any degree of comfort.

The section boss at Anginita told me that men were wanted out at a place called Del Norte, some few miles west of here, so seeing nothing going on in the country that I could take a hand at, I went there, was hired at once, and again became a section hand. The wages here were a dollar and a half a day ; we had to pay four dollars fifty cents for board. I worked at this place for the next two months and a half. Nothing of any interest happened here, but a short distance away, near a place called Garland, there was a murder. That would have been nothing of itself, as murders are quite common in Colorado ; but this particular case was of particular interest owing to the fact that the victim, a Mexican farmer, was much liked by all who knew him. It appeared that his wife had seen some man whom she liked better than she did her husband,

and the two of them made up their minds to remove him. Accordingly one day, when he was
hitching up his team, this strange man shot him
with a Colt's revolver, inflicting two wounds, one
through each lung. However, though mortally
wounded, he had strength enough left to draw his
weapon and inflict a wound on his assailant that
necessited the amputation of his right forearm.
The farmer lived, I believe, for 48 hours; however he lived long enough to make it only murder
in the second degree, for which reason they did not
hang the murderer, but only gave him six years in
the penitentiary at Cañon City. This penitentiary
is said to be the most severe in the United States,
and a man here told me that to get a term of six or
seven years at it was in reality worse than being
hanged, as no ordinary man could possibly survive
it. " For," said he, " if a man has the constitution
of a steer, or of a grizzly bear, the kind of work
they put him to there at all seasons of the year will
break it down in a very short time."

This being the case, perhaps the punishment was
severe enough for the crime. And to tell the truth,
so far as I have heard, the penitentiaries, or some of
them, in the United States are harder than any in
the world. I have often spoken to tramps who had
been in the houses of correction, and they were
horribly afraid of getting there again. Often they
will go round a circuit of many miles to escape
even the slightest chance of getting put on the

"rock-pile" as they call it. Policemen, too, in America are very severe and even brutal in the way they treat men; and some of the laws in this free country are such as would make Englishmen think of a new revolution. I found this out afterwards for myself. The woman who was in this case came in for a sentence of two years' imprisonment on account of her share in this transaction.

While I was at this place I took it into my head to go down to Denver, and I stayed there for a day or two. It is a fine city with tramcars, theatres, electric lights, and so on, and is situated in a great basin of the mountains. My object in going there was to see if there was any probability of obtaining any work of a less rough or more lucrative nature than that at which I was engaged, but seeing no likelihood of getting any I returned to my job on the section, where I stayed for another month. About this time I became acquainted with a man who went by the name of Bunk Redman, a Missourian, and he suggested that I and he should go out on the Silverton branch to a place called Durango, where he had been before and where, according to his account, there was plenty of work and good wages. Not liking my present occupation, and being ready by this time for a change, I agreed to go. I sold my time for a dollar less than it was worth to one of the men in the gang and we started out.

On this journey I saw the celebrated Toltec gorge ; I will not attempt to describe it for I could not, it is a thing that must be seen to be understood. This much I will say, and that is, that far as I have travelled—and I have travelled a great deal even for this age of quick transit—I never saw it surpassed for rugged grandeur.

Arriving at Durango we did not find things quite as glorious as we had anticipated. There certainly was work, but the wages were not very high. Bunk soon procured a job to drive a six-mule team for which he got sixty dollars a month, but I had to look further, not being up to taking that kind of work. After doing nothing for two days, I at last decided to go to work at the coke ovens : here we worked in eight hour shifts and got $2. 50 c. a shift. Every one on this job boarded where he liked best, there being no boarding establishment attached to the place. I worked here for about two weeks and then left, owing to a dispute I had one day with the boss. I obtained work the same day in a planing mill at the same wages. I continued at this job most of the rest of the time I remained in Durango.

During this time some of my chums in Durango organised a hunting expedition, as there was not much to do in town and most of us had been working all the summer and had a few dollars by us. I was invited to join in and go out with them for a few days, of course bearing my share of the expenses and sharing in the profits if there were any. A couple of pack-mules were hired to carry our baggage and provisions. I was totally unacquainted with the country about here, and was in consequence entirely in the hands of the others of the party, who all knew something about it. There were three besides myself, all young men, and we made a rather jolly party, as the expedition was as much one of pleasure as business, and we travelled by easy stages, always selecting as comfortable camping places as could be found.

On the afternoon of the third day we were camped on the sloping side of a mountain in such a position as to have a clear view down a wide valley which was tolerably clear of scrub. All at once one of the boys, by name Hoskins, said there were some deer in the valley below us. I looked in the direction pointed out, and saw some animals, but could not be certain that they were deer, as the distance was at least 1,000 yards, and they were standing amongst some light scrub. I told Hoskins I was by no means sure that they were deer. He only laughed at me, and said that as I had not been in the mountains any time, it was not to be expected I could know anything about the matter—the justice of which remark I was quite ready to acknowledge. " Any way, here goes for a shot at them !" said he, as he took his rifle, and got down comfortably in the back position as if he was at target practice, for he had been in the American army and had qualified as a sharpshooter. Bang

went the first shot, but nothing stirred; he adjusted
his sights and fired again, when I saw one of them
go down. The other two fellows were standing by
and they now urged Hoskins on, saying " Shove in
another cartridge, man! don't move! You have
got the range now and you can get another." He
let fly again, with the result that another one came
down, but still no movement was perceptible
amongst the rest of the herd. Hoskins now sat up
with rather a grave look on his face, and said,
" Look here, boys, there is something wrong in this,
deer do not stand up in a bunch to be shot down
that way, I think it would be as well to investigate
this matter before going any further." Accordingly
we all went down to see the game, and were not a
little disgusted to find two burros (as they call the
Mexican donkey) lying dead, and three more
standing round and appearing to be in no way
concerned in what was going on. Hoskins and Co.
looked pretty foolish about this, but I refrained
from saying, " I told you so," which under the
circumstances was, I think, rather to my credit. We
stayed out for about two weeks altogether, during
which time I had my first shot at a big cinnamon
bear, and if it had not been for the assistance I got
from the others I should in all likelihood have
fallen a prey to the savage beast, for I was not up
to the business and fired at him when he had the
rising ground and a clear run right to where I
stood. This would not have mattered much if I had

given him a bad wound first shot, but I had only cut the hide on his shoulder and hurt him just enough to make him properly savage. I had no idea till now that a bear could travel so fast, but this one was all of 300 yards from me when I fired, and before I could say "knife" he was within about 50 yards, and coming straight for me with his mouth open and eyes glaring with rage. I stood there quite stupefied, as the cartridge I had just fired had stuck in my rifle, and jerk as I would on the lever, I could not move it. This mishap would most certainly have cost me my life if it had not happened that Hoskins was in sight all the time, and had seen the thing from the start, and now, with one of the others, came to my assistance with a couple of well-directed shots from behind me, which laid Bruin out just in his hour of triumph. The accident to my rifle was a trifling one in ordinary circumstances, but with such a dangerous customer as a wounded cinnamon bear to deal with, it would, without the timely assistance I got from my companions, have proved fatal to me.

CHAPTER VII.

From the Land of Snow.

It was towards the middle of December that my partner, Bunk Redman, came in from the country where he had been working, hauling logs to a sawmill with a six-mule team, but as the mill was now shut down on account of the severity of the weather he was out of a job. Some little time before this I had received a letter from my brother Morley, in which he informed me that he was coming out to Texas in a short time. As the mill I was working at was then about to shut down, I made up my mind to go down to Texas and see if I could locate myself somewhere so that I could write and let my brother know where he would find me. Speaking one day to Bunk on this subject, he said, "if we intend to get out of here this winter we want to make a start as soon as possible, or we shall likely enough be snowed in, as this branch of the road is often snowed up entirely for months at a time; and although there is not much snow just here the mountain passes must be pretty bad even now." "If that is the case," said I, "I am going by to-night's train, for I have

no particular wish to stay here sucking my thumbs
for three months." To this Bunk agreed at once,
as he had made a pretty good stake, and wanted
to go east for the winter.

The train left Durango just before midnight, and
as there happened to be no one but ourselves in
the carriage we managed to make ourselves very
comfortable, and slept till morning. There had
been very little snow on the ground at Durango,
but now everything was covered feet deep with it
and we were making slow and laborious progress
up the divide. There was a snow plough with two
engines to it " bucking the snow " (as the expression
goes here) in front of us, and we followed in her
wake with another plough, of course on the engine
that was drawing the train. There had been a
gang of 50 snow shovellers on the train when we
left, or they had been picked up somewhere while
I was asleep. These men were employed cutting
the snow drifts down at each side of the track to
give the snow plough a chance to break up the
masses of it that were piled on the track, and throw
it to either side. This gang was increased at every
place we came to, for wherever the train men could
pick up a " bum " they did so and gave him a
shovel, so that by the time we passed " Chama,"
which is nearly on the top of the Conejos divide
(where we passed the west-bound train), we had in
all three locomotives, two snow ploughs, and a gang
of 75 snow shovellers to help us along ; and yet for

some hours it seemed to me, and indeed I think to everyone else, that it was doubtful if we should succeed in getting through. However, we did manage it, and when we began to descend the other side of the range, the snow, both that which was falling and that which had accumulated on the ground, decreased at every mile, till the track was once more comparatively clear. Henceforward, fair progress was made for the last part of the journey, which ended for me at Angineta, where the Española branch joined the road. This was my way, for I was going down through New Mexico.

Here I parted with Bunk Redman, and have never seen him since. I found to my disgust, on making inquiries, that one of the two weekly trains that ran on this branch had gone that afternoon, and there were three days to wait for the next. I at once made up my mind to walk (the distance, as I mentioned before, was 92 miles); but it being now late in the afternoon it was no use starting that night.

Going to the solitary boarding-house I asked what would be the charge for supper, bed, and breakfast, and was coolly informed that it would be $3. I argued and expostulated with the boss, but to no purpose; he knew that he had me foul, as they say in fighting, and would not come back a cent, so I was perforce obliged to pay it. At this piece of barefaced robbery, for it was nothing else, I was very mad, but could not help myself. Next

morning after breakfast, which consisted of rusty
pork and black beans with some doughy bread and
stinking butter and coffee like muddy water, I
started out on my walk. There was no need to
carry water as there was plenty of snow on the
ground, but determining not to be victimised any
more by a thief of a boarding-house keeper, I took
no food with me, determining to get some at Tres
Piedres if I could not manage to procure some at
any of the section-houses on the road. I had to
walk along the railroad track, as that was the only
road as far as I knew, and in any case it would be
the nearest.

There was just snow enough on the ground to
make it very bad walking indeed; the ties were
covered so that I could not see properly which
place to step on. The consequence of this was that
I soon began to miss my footing and fall. This
kind of thing went on all day, till late in the
afternoon I came to the first section-house and
asked to be allowed to stay there that night,
offering to pay for what they gave me. But the
only person who was in the house was a vinegary-
looking woman, who told me that I could not stay;
she also resolutely refused to give or sell me the
smallest scrap of food, and telling me there was
another house nine miles further on, she banged the
door in my face and I heard her securing it on the
inside. When a man has been travelling over a
bad road all day with nothing to eat, it is rather

hard lines to be turned away from shelter and coolly told to go nine miles more, with the possible prospect of being treated the same way when he gets there. However, there was no help for it, so I made another start, cursing everything on earth, but particularly the inhospitable beast of a woman who was the cause of my trouble. It was now getting dark, and to make things still more unpleasant, the snow began to fall in big soft flakes, and soon there was as heavy a snowstorm as I ever saw. I could not see my hand in front of my face, and the snow being soft, was as bad as rain. Not being able to see, I of course made very poor progress, and, many times missing my footing, I rolled right down the bank into the ditch, which was filled with slushy snow and in some places with water. The consequence of this was that I was soon wet through and bruised from head to foot from my falls amongst the rocks. Tired and aching in every limb, and wet through, I stumbled along, looking for anything in the shape of a light that should guide me to the house I was expecting to see. At last, when I was beginning to think I must have passed it, I saw a faint glimmer of light, and going up to it, I found that it was the other section-house.

Now, remembering the reception I had received at the last place, I resolved I would either get what I wanted here or I would inaugurate a funeral either for myself or somebody else; I did not care much which. So unbuttoning my coat I pulled my six-shooter round handy over my right hip and knocked at the door. But my warlike preparations were needless, as my reception here was a good as it had been bad at the other place. It was half-past eleven when I arrived, and it must have been about four o'clock when I was turned away from the last place, so it had taken me seven hours and a half to walk nine miles; this alone should give some idea of the sort of a time I had been having.

The man who opened the door to me was the section boss, and a very good fellow indeed he turned out to be. "Come in," said he, "you look as if you had been having an interesting time; how far have you travelled to-day?" He then threw some more wood in the stove, and telling me to take all my clothes off, he went out of the room, saying he would go and hunt me up some of his to put on till my own were dry.

When he came back with the clothes he remarked that the old woman (*i.e.* his wife) was in bed, but he would get me something to eat, which he did. While I was eating what he gave me he went out and bringing in an armful of blankets told me to make up a bed by the stove and turn in when I was ready.

In the morning I put on my own clothes again, which were now dry. After breakfast I pulled out my pocket-book and asked what I owed, but the boss would take nothing, saying that he was glad to be able to do a man a good turn now and then. I told him of the kind reception I had got at the other house, at which he said, " Oh! I know her well enough, she ought to be kicked all round the house every twenty minutes and get double allowance on Sundays and public holidays." This treatment would have been I think rather too severe even for her offence, though if it had been in my power to inflict it on her the previous night I should most certainly have done so.

There had been a sharp frost that morning, and though much colder it was on the whole a great deal better travelling than it had been the previous day ; the snowstorm had ceased and the sky was most beautifully clear. The whole landscape was covered with snow as far as the eye could reach, and the ragged lines of snow-covered mountain peaks which bounded the view on either hand and rose up behind me, looked as if they might have been painted on a background of pale blue sky. By pushing on as fast as the nature of the travelling would permit I had no doubt of being able to make Tres Piedres before night. This I did, and even earlier than I had hoped to.

At some time or other this place was a mining camp, but whatever had brought it into existence had either been worked out or found not profitable enough to go on working, for it was now deserted. This was good luck for me, as it had again begun to snow so heavily that I determined to camp till it either cleared off or the train came along. The train would be due on the afternoon of the next day, and if the weather did not improve in the meantime I meant to go by it. The first thing I did was to go over to the deserted mining camp and pick out the best house there to camp in. I selected one that had a mud chimney and fireplace. There was a good roof on it, and although the door and window had been removed there was no great amount of snow in it, owing to the fact that they were both on the lee side of the house. After deciding on staying here, I went round some of the other houses and getting what loose wood I could find I made a fire, and hanging my blanket over the window I had a good warm. Having now fixed up my camp, as far as the means at my disposal would permit, I went over to the depôt and saw the agent, from whom I bought some bread and a piece of beef. Returning to my camp I cut a bit of beef and roasted it on the hot coals and made a good meal, which I washed down with a drink of melted snow. It was now drawing on towards evening, and just as I was thinking of turning in three waggons and a buggy came up to the place with five or six Mexican men and three women. They seemed to expect to find an inhabited town, but as none of them spoke English I could not find out what they wanted. I took them to be a Mexican family moving with their household goods to some other part of the country.

The women seemed to be a mother and her two daughters. One thing about the outfit struck me as peculiar, and that was that as far as I could see none of the men were armed, nor did I see them take any arms from the waggons. I noticed that they eyed me rather suspiciously, more especially the women, and I certainly looked a rough enough character. I was dressed in a complete suit of California ducks, rather the worse for wear, with cowhide boots to my knees, and a broad-brimmed felt hat, while round my waist I wore a leather cartridge belt full of ammunition, in which I carried a good serviceable Colt's revolver ; add to this that my hair was long and ragged, that I had not shaved for about three weeks, nor washed my face for the last four days, and I have no doubt that my appearance was not reassuring. However, as these people had come to my camp, I felt in a manner bound to be hospitable as far as my means went, which I need not say was not far. I did what I could to reassure them and make them understand that I was not a road agent or desperado, which I was beginning to think they took me for. I assisted the men to unhitch their horses after I had piled more wood on the fire, and indicated to the ladies to take up their quarters in the corner that I had intended to sleep in myself ; for this piece of civility they did not appear to be duly thankful. Then I showed the men where there was a house that would make a good stable. After that I could do no more but

show them that there was a store at the depôt
where they could procure anything they happened
to need.   However, they had a good camping outfit
with them and soon made themselves as comfortable
as they could.   One of the men went over to the store
to get something, and when he came back he said
something to the others, and at once they seemed
to regard me in a more favourable light.   One of
the girls, who by the way was very pretty, came
over to where I was sitting and gave me a cup of
coffee, some of which they had just been brewing.
Shortly after the depôt agent came over and
explained the mystery.   It appeared that he could
talk Spanish, and that the man who went over to
the store had asked him who I was, expressing at
the same time his conviction that I was not a
character to be trusted; but on the agent telling
him that he knew me, and that I was merely a
harmless traveller going about my own business, he
became reassured, and coming over communicated
the good news to the rest, which accounted for
their altered manner to me.

CHAPTER VIII.

Hitting the Road.

It was still snowing pretty hard when I woke up in the early morning and looked out. But in spite of this, and the want of any indications that the weather would clear up, the Mexicans harnessed their team and pulled out of camp.

This was neither the first nor last time that I met Mexicans, and sometimes I was not very glad of their company, for they do not bear the very best character for honesty, and most Western Americans believe they will cut a man's throat for half a dollar, if they suspect him of having as much about him ; but if they think any one is very poor they are often good to him, and will give him food and shelter. As a general rule they are very easy-going, not fond of too much work, but good tempered if they are not interfered with. Though a few of them are desperadoes, yet, as I have said, this party at Tres Piedres seemed a deal more afraid of me than I was of them.

As the weather was still so bad I made up my mind to stay where I was until the train came

along. I had nothing to do and could sleep no
more, so I went over to the house and had a yarn
with the depôt agent, who told me a rather good
story about a man who had been a sailor who
undertook to drive a bullock cart. It appears he
knew nothing about bullocks, so when he came to
the hill down which he had to go to get to the
house, he climbed on his load instead of putting
the brake on. The heavy weight made the bullocks
run, and they finally capsized the cart at the
bottom, sending him flying. The two women ran
out and found him lying there knocked rather
stupid. " Run, run " said one to the other, " perhaps he isn't killed ; bring the brandy and a spoon."
This roused the patient and in a tone of great
contempt he murmured " Spoon, spoon ? Oh, hang
it ! bring a cup."

So between yarning with this agent and smoking
and chewing over his hot stove, I put in a good
spell of time. When I left him I wandered round
the deserted huts and old ruins of the mining camp,
which was now so quiet.

It was well on in the afterooon when the train
I was waiting for arrived. When I got away it was
snowing. The fare which I paid was, I believe,
four dollars, and this expenditure brought me down
rather low in pocket. Still I expected to be able to
beat my way when I got down on the Atchisin,
Topeka, and Santa Fé railroad, where trains were
more plentiful, and the conductors and brakesmen

less likely to have nothing to do but hunt for dead-beats and put them off.

As we were now leaving the higher country the grade was downhill all the way, and consequently the snow soon fell as rain when we left the hills where it was still lying. This part of the country was very thinly populated; towns there were none, and consequently we made good time through not having to stop. We reached Española about mid-night. I was the only passenger on the train. For some time before our arrival I had seen clusters of small fires dotting the mountain sides in all directions, but was at a loss to make out what they were. On arriving at Española I noticed that every house in the place had a little fire in front of the door. On inquiring what this meant I was told that it was a custom of the Mexicans to keep a fire burning in front of their house all Christmas Eve. So it was Christmas Eve and I never knew it.

There was no snow here, but in spite of that it was very cold; so after getting some supper, for which I had to pay fifty cents, I was obliged to fork out fifty more for a bed. Thus my stock of money was reduced by a dollar. The stage that ran between this place and Santa Fé started at nine next morning, but as the fare was six dollars I did not see my way clear to going by it, till the driver who heard me making the inquiries called me on one side, and said, " Old man, I do not like to see a man in a fix, so if you will walk out on the road

a mile or so I will pick you up if you choose to put
up a couple of dollars, and you can get off just
before we arrive in Santa Fé." Judging it best to
get over this part of the road as quickly as possible,
I closed with his offer, and rode instead of walking.
We had a spanking team of four horses, so that we
made good time in spite of the roughness of the
road, and half-way we stopped at a ranch and
changed horses. The air was mild and yet bracing.
The mountain scenery in places was very fine, and
I enjoyed the drive immensely. This was altogether
better travelling than the way I came up in the
spring.

This was Christmas Day, and taking everything
into account it was not the worst I ever spent. I
thought I would like to go to my old employer
at the store, but it being Christmas Day the store
was shut up, and I did not consider that I
presented a good enough appearance to go up to
his private house. So I went and paid my friend
Pistol Johnny a visit, but finding him very drunk
and apparently quarrelsome I did not speak to
him. But his wife recognised me, and asked
how I was, which was as far as her politeness
went.

The train for Lamy Junction did not start till
eight o'clock that night, so I had an hour or two on
my hands, and did not know very well how to put
it in. I strolled about the town and went into
several gambling saloons and watched the play,

which was chiefly faro and Spanish monté, though a few poker games were being well patronised. There was also a wheel of fortune for those who did not possess any skill at the other games. At last the time came to go down to the depôt, and I was very glad of it, for I was tired of loafing about the town. I had to shell out another dollar for the journey down to Lamy. For this I was sorry, but there was no help for it, as the trains are watched so closely here that there is no chance to beat them. At Lamy the people at the hotel gave me supper and accommodated me with sleeping room on the floor, for which they charged me nothing as it was Christmas, and they were having a good time. They had a Christmas tree here, and the mistress of the house gave me a gingerbread cow, for she said that as it was Christmas every one in her house must have a present of some kind. Next morning I counted up what money I had, and found it only came to five dollars, and I had set my mind on going as far at least as Big Springs, Texas. This was very little money to go that distance on. As I was waiting about for a train to come along a man came up to me and asked if I wanted to sell my revolver. I did not like to do it, but get to Big Springs I must somehow or other, and for this I required a little money; so I sold him the revolver, scabbard, and belt for twelve dollars; this was about half what it was worth, but he would give no more.

Shortly after this a train came along, and not being able to get into a car, I jumped up between two of them and rode on the draw heads as far as Wallace, which was the end of that division. I got off without being observed, but when she pulled out again I was spotted and could not get away. I waited here some time till a coal train came into the depôt. I jumped it, and got as far as Algodones, but just before arriving at this place the conductor and head brakesman spotted me, and coming out of the caboose they pelted me with lumps of coal, but did not hit me. However, when we pulled up at the station I got off, not caring to furnish a target for the train-men to fire lumps of coal at. Here I jumped another train, and got " bounced " at Bernalillo. This was not making good progress, but I determined that if I got bounced twenty times a day I would not put up a cent to a breaky again. I could not manage to get away from here this day, and at night I slept in an empty box-car that was standing on a siding. The next morning I was more fortunate, for while a freight train was switched off here waiting for the mail to pass the train-men were regaling themselves in a beer saloon, and taking advantage of their absence I opened the tool box under the caboose, and finding there was room for me I got in, getting a half-breed Indian that was loafing about there to shut-to the door. For this I gave him a piece of tobacco. I managed to get as far as Albuquerque this time, and should have got down to San Marcial, which is the end of that division, but the train-men wanted some tools for something or other, and when they came for them of course I was found and invited to come out. After that I tried two or three freights here, but with no success. So when the west-bound passenger came through that night I jumped on the cow-catcher, and was fortunate enough to get as far as Socorro, and should have been able to go a good way further only it was so cold in my exposed position that I got off and began to look about for some place to camp. I found the smouldering remains of a camp fire in a dry ditch which was fairly well sheltered ; so throwing the embers together, I fanned it into a blaze with my hat, and collecting a few pieces of wood and coal I found lying about, I rolled myself in my blanket and went to sleep.

Next morning when I woke I went up to the town, which lay some little distance from the railroad. Here I found out that there was a railroad just going to be commenced out to the Socorro mines, which are situated in the Magdalena mountains, a few miles to the westward of the town of Socorro. The consequence of this was that the town was full of all the bums in the country, who said that they were waiting for the work to commence, though I very much doubt if 20 per cent. of the whole crowd would have gone to work at anything at all if they had it offered to them.

A more villainous gang of ragamuffins I do not think I ever saw ; in fact I liked their looks so little that although I had money in my pocket, and I was as hungry as a wolf, I would not change any for fear some of them might get to know I had it. I am quite sure that if some of the roughs that were lying around that town knew that I had any money I should not have got away with any of it if they could help it. So I looked about to find some way of getting some food, but for some time could find nothing ; but at last a man came and asked me if I would give him a hand to get a cook stove into a shanty where he was going to set up a " hash house." I helped him and he gave me something to eat as payment. While I was here I got talking to a man who owned a team and was waiting for the railroad operations to commence. He was well acquainted with the place and the surrounding country, where he had been for some time. He said to me " You see that affair on the hill over yonder ? Well, that is the Billings smelter ; it is a lead smelter, and they are short-handed up there. You are sure to be asked to go to work, but don't you do it. If you should make up your mind to do so, just get some one to lend you a gun and blow your brains out first, it will save you a lot of trouble." I asked him why he was so down on the job, and he said that the country was full of poor devils who had been poisoned through and through .with the lead fumes, and who he asserted would never be any good again. On making further inquiries I found that he was to a great extent correct in what he stated, that the ore which came from the Magdalena mines was of a peculiarly bad nature, being what is termed amongst miners white carbonate ore, and amongst other impurities it was said to contain a large percentage of arsenic, but of this I can assert nothing positively. I was told that a teamster who was employed in taking the stuff from the mines to the smelter one night when the ground was wet camped on top of his load, and in the morning he was lead-poisoned so badly that he was under medical treatment for some months.

Not caring for the look of the place, and being anxious to push on, I left that night on the passenger. There was a sharp frost, and it was so cold that I had to look out for a warm corner, so I jumped the hind end of the sleeper. We were no sooner off than the sleeping car porter came out and wanted to know what I was doing there; but I satisfied his scruples with half a dollar and he let me alone for the rest of the time I was on the train. When we arrived at San Marcial it was so cold that I decided not to go any further. Here I met with an accident that delayed me for 10 days besides costing me nearly all the money I had. It was pitch dark, and as I was walking across the yard I stumbled and struck my right knee against a switch lever, and hurt it so much that travelling was out of the question till it got better. So I put

up at the hotel, which cost me a dollar a day. The
next morning, instead of being any better, it was
worse and much swollen. There was a man here who
called himself a doctor ; so being frightened that I
might have injured my knee more that I at first
thought, I went to him. He gave a bottle of stuff for
which he charged me two dollars. I believe it was
just common turpentine liniment and worth about
ten cents. I soon saw that there was nothing very
serious the matter, but was too stiff and sore to
move about for ten days. Though the place was
dull enough most of the time that I was in this
condition, there was one thing happened while I
was there that created quite a little sensation. As
I was sitting on the piazza of the house at which I
was staying I noticed a man come riding up the
street and get off his horse in front of a small
saloon that was situated about a couple of ·hundred
yards from where I was. He was dressed in the
usual cow-boy rig of that region and rode a small
broncho pony. Almost at the same moment that
he entered the house I heard three pistol shots in
quick succession, and he came out of the saloon
again, and mounting his pony, he swam it across
the river, and rode away in the direction of the
Organ mountains.

Knowing by this time quite enough of the
country to be aware that for men to shoot each
other was a comparatively common occurrence and
considered by the bulk of the population, if not

altogether a commendable exploit, at least justified
by what most people in Europe would consider
altogether insufficient provocation, I thought it
not at all unlikely that there were some dead men
in that saloon. I accordingly got up and walked
over to see. I was not wrong in my supposition, for
the first thing I saw when I entered was two men
lying under the pool table, one shot through the
middle of the forehead and quite dead, while the
other was lying face down; but on turning him
over I found he was shot in the breast and also
quite dead. The bartender was lying in one corner
behind the bar, shot through the right lung and
mortally wounded; he died the same night.

Three men shot in broad daylight in the middle
of a town could not be overlooked altogether, so
some of the citizens saddled up and went in pursuit
or pretended to, but they put it off till the murderer
had got such a start as to make it almost a certainty that he would not be caught, at that time any
way. I found out that this was the outcome of a
gambling row that had occurred a night or two
before, when this man had accused one of the three
dead men of cheating, and had been rather roughly
handled by them.

My knee was still very stiff and sore when I
made a start, but I was down to my last dollar,
and so could not have stayed if I had wished. I
jumped a freight here, and not being able to get
into a car I rode the drawheads down to a place a

few miles north of Rincon Junction. From this
place the branch line runs down to El Paso, Texas.
Where I was was no more than a small way
station and would be a bad place to get away from,
so I decided to walk. I arrived at Rincon about
ten o'clock at night. It was freezing hard and
miserably cold. Here I found about half a dozen
men who were on the road as well as myself. They
were camped in an old log house where they had a
big coal fire blazing on a mud hearth at one end of
the place. They seemed to be very comfortable, so
I joined the company and selecting a vacant spot
I lay down on the floor and was soon asleep. It
was just grey dawn when I was awakened by some
of the others who said the place was on fire, and
on getting up I saw that this was the case. The
fire had already got such a hold that I could see
that there was not much chance of putting it out.
Every one was suggesting something; one said
throw dirt on it, another said pull the burning logs
out, while one man volunteered to go and fetch
water, which he did, but it was only a small
salmon tin full. When he arrived with this valu-
able fire-extinguishing appliance he stood for a few
moments looking at the fire and then, slowly raising
the tin to his lips, he drank the water, and throwing
the tin into the fire he said, "Which is the way to
Deming, we had better get out of this before the
citizens come and run us out." Not knowing how
the owner of the shanty might take the burning of

it, I thought it as well to take this hint and make myself scarce, but as I wanted to stay at this place till I could get a train down to El Paso I could not go away altogether. So I simply walked back on the track for about a mile, and waiting till the sun was well up, I then returned as if I had not been there before. When I got back I found a crowd of people looking at the smouldering remains of the house and cursing the "bums," as they termed them, who had set it on fire. As I was coming in from the east and went up to have a look, no one ever suspected that I knew anything about it, nor did I see fit to let them know that I did. I stayed here all this day and had nothing to eat as I had only 35 cents, and would not spend it till I was absolutely obliged. Some time in the afternoon a freight came along and switched off on to the branch, and I was fortunate enough to be able to stow myself away in a car that was partly filled with baled hay. This was a very comfortable ride indeed, but I did not hold it far, for while I was asleep they switched the car out at a place called Las Cruces. When I awoke and found the car at a standstill I had a look out. Though it was night-time and quite dark I at once took in the situation, and cursing my luck turned in again and slept till morning. When daylight came I found that my lodging was shared by a strange man whom I had not seen before. Of course we at once struck up an acquaintance, and he told me that he was going down into Texas in the hopes of being able to get some work there. He added that this was the morning of the third day since ho had had anything to eat. He was not a professional tramp I could see ; his hands were hard and scarred with work, and his clothes were such as are usually worn by miners. I told him, in return for his information, I was nearly as bad as himself, having eaten nothing for the last 24 hours. He then said we must have a look round and see if we could manage to get something. After strolling round the place, which is only a village, for awhile, we spotted some very fine turkeys, and my hungry companion said at once, "There is a good feed for two mon ou one of those jokers ; we must have one of them, but we must wait till after dark, it will not do to take them in broad daylight." However, as I still had a few cents I did not feel justified in stealing turkeys, so I told him that I had 10 cents and would spend it in bread if we could find any for sale. All the people in the place seemed to be Mexicans, but at last wo came to a shanty where a Chinaman had a kind of a store. From him I bought 10 cents worth of bread, but put all together there was not enough to satisfy one of us. However, I cut it in two and giving the other fellow half I ate the rest myself. This, be it understood, was about nine o'clock in the forenoon. There being nothing for us to do, at least not till dark, if my new partner kept to his intention, we went down to the railway again.

The car in which we had arrived was now empty, someone having come and taken the hay away, so our bed was gone. However, the car was a shelter and the air was keen, so we took up our quarters there for the present. I lay down in one corner and tried to go to sleep, for when a man is asleep he does not feel hunger, and I always think that when there is little food to be had it is as well to keep as still as possible ; it prevents to a certain extent getting hungry, I believe. At last I succeeded, and it was late in the day when I woke and found my chum was not in the car. He soon came back, however, and said to me, "You stood breakfast, I am going to find something for supper." I asked him where he proposed to get it. "Never mind," said he, "I will get it or bust in the attempt." He then told me to go along the side of the track and pick up what pieces of coal I could find. Without asking any more questions I did as I was requested, and in the course of an hour or so had quite a good pile, besides some pieces of wood.

I had a pretty good notion that he meant to have a turkey, but any scruples of conscience I may have had on this score in the morning were fast disappearing under the pressure of circumstances, for I was getting most desperately hungry. My partner (whose name I did not trouble to inquire) had a look at the fuel, and said that it would be enough for his purpose. He then communicated to me that he had a kerosine tin planted all right,

that would just suit what he wanted it for, which
he now avowed was to capture, cook, and eat one
of the turkeys we had seen in the morning. He had
found out where they camped, and as soon as they
retired for the night and things were quiet about
the town he went and captured one. In the meantime I had put some water in the tin, and had it on
the fire boiling when he came back with the turkey.
It did not take long to dress, for I soused it into
the boiling water feathers and all; by doing this
the feathers all came off with a rub, and as they
were wet they did not fly about, thus making it
much easier to conceal the evidences of our horrible
crime. We were so hungry and the turkey smelt
so good that he never got the chance to get
properly cooked, for we were hooking pieces of it
out and scalding our fingers and mouths with it
long before it was half done; in fact the cooking
and eating processes went on at the same time, and
both came to an end at the same time.

After we had finished our meal we dug a hole in
the sand and buried the bones and feathers, and as
luck would have it we got away that night the
same way as we got left the night before, for a
train came along and picked up our empty and took
us down to El Paso, where we arrived early next
morning. This was a piece of very good fortune,
for we might have been run up north again instead
of going in the direction we wanted. Here I parted
with my companion, who got a job at something or

other in one of the railway shops. There was not much going on in this town, and the weather was most abominably cold. The wind was blowing what they call a " norther," a real " Texas norther," and a beautiful thing it was. The locomotives were smothered from one end to the other with frozen steam. The wheels were in most cases just like discs of ice, and there were icicles as thick as a man's leg hanging from the underside of the cylinders, and anywhere else where there was a leak of either steam or water.

I wandered round the town for a while very disconsolately, but at last I sat down on a seat in the plaza, and near to me came and sat down a couple of tramps, real bonâ fide " bums." There was no mistake about them, for they were ragged and filthy beyond description. They addressed each other as " pard," although, as far as I could gather from their conversation, they had only just met by chance that morning. Bum No. 1. said to his companion, " Say, pard, done any chewing lately?" " No," said he, " I ain't; this town is about bummed out, and it ain't safe to ask for anything; the cops are on to me already, and I must shift soon, or I am good for the chain-gang." " Well, you come along with me," said No. 1. " I saw a man plant some bread and bacon in a prairie dog hole this morning, and if he has not taken it away again we will go and get it. It ain't much, but it is better than risking the chain-gang."

They got up and walked away, and that was the last I saw of them, though no doubt they went away and got the prize they were speaking of. But their conversation set me thinking that I was very hungry too, and as I had nothing "cached" in a prairie dog hole I hunted up a restaurant kept by a Chinaman, to whom I gave my last quarter for a meal. So I was once more "busted," and added another to my long list of bankruptcies. I started at once to look for a train, and as El Paso is rather a large place, with a good many people about the depôt and railroad yards, I determined to go out to the first station on the road east and wait there for a freight train instead of attempting to board one at the city. Ysleta was the name of the place I came to; it was a rather pretty little Mexican village. When I got there there was some kind of a festival going on, and the people, in spite of the cold weather, seemed to be enjoying themselves in good style. Having nothing to do till a train came by I went to work to find some shelter, and after rummaging round for a while I came across a dug-out that was in pretty fair condition, and had some straw in one corner. This straw had a rather musty smell, and looked as if it had furnished a bed for some generations of tramps. However, I was by this time learning to be thankful for small mercies. My first move was to get some fuel and make a fire, and as there was plenty of coal lying about the track which had I suppose fallen from the locomotive tenders and coal trains, I soon had a fire under way that would have roasted an ox. I thought it unfortunate that I had not a portion of one to roast, but I gave myself a good roasting instead. I now lay down on the straw, and as it was not more than supper time I did not feel very hungry, having had some dinner this day, so I was rather jolly as times went then. I had not been here long, and was just beginning to get drowsy, when a man came in and asked me which way I was travelling. On my telling him that I was going east, he said, "There will be an east-bound freight here in a minute or two, and she is sure to stop, as there are some empties on the siding." I asked him if he had ever been on this road before, and he said he had. It was, according to his account, the easiest road in the States to get over as the train-men never troubled anyone. "But," added he, "there is a very good-chance of getting killed, as there is a wreck of some sort on this line about three times a week on an average."

As he was speaking the freight he had told me of drew up, and picked up the empties, into one of which I and my chance acquaintance jumped. I was loath to leave my good fire, but I wanted to get on my road, and could not afford to lose a chance. The cold this night was intense, and the car was full of cracks through which the wind whistled in draughts that seemed to go right through one. I danced and jumped and thrashed my arms to try and keep life in myself, but in spite of all I could do the tears were running down my face with the cold. I do not mean to say that I was crying, but I have noticed on many occasions, when exposed to intense cold, that the water would run from my eyes in a very annoying fashion, for by continually wiping my eyes I made them quite sore. I travelled all that night, and early in the morning came to a place called Sierra Blanca. I was now regularly done up with the fatigue of vainly trying to keep myself warm, for in spite of all my exercise I was almost half frozen. There was no town here, though there was an eating establishment at the depôt, which of course did me no good as I had no money.

There is no natural water here, and all water has to be brought from a distance on the train. There is an artesian well that throws up a continual large stream of water, but it is unfit to drink, and so bad that it cannot be used in the boilers of the locomotives. It has a faint bluish tinge, and the people here warned me not to drink any, as they said it was poison. The thing cost the railroad some thousands of dollars to bore, as I was told. It is nearly all the way through rock, and 1,500 feet deep. There was no train till late in the evening, and I should have had nothing to eat if a good-natured brakesman who was there had not given me what he had left over from his own dinner.

CHAPTER IX.

On the T.P.

In the evening I got on the freight train bound east without any trouble and so left Sierra Blanca. My next stay was at Big Springs. During this part of the journey I found that what my last partner had said was quite true. The Texas Pacific was, compared with most other lines that I knew, very easy to beat. The train-men were very good fellows indeed. I was in an empty box car, or tramps " side door Pullman," and found it very cold for the sides were full of cracks. I walked up and down and thrashed my arms to keep warm, but it was very difficult to do so. At last the train stopped at a place called Wild Horse, and the front brakesman came down my way to something or other. As he passed my car he opened the door, swung his lamp in, and seeing me said, " Cold travelling this, old man, why don't you get out of here and ride on the engine ?" This was a surprise to me, as I rather expected to get put off, as I had no money to give him to be allowed to stay. So I said that I guessed the engineer would have something to say to that, and that I should not be allowed to. He then sung out to the engineer, and told him about me. This man at once called me, and told me that I was quite welcome to come and ride there with him as far as he went, which was to Big Springs, the end of the division. This engineer was about as kindly a fellow as I ever met. After asking me some questions, where I was going, and what I intended to do, he shared his supper with me, making me eat the biggest share, and giving me some hot tea, a luxury I had not seen for some time. He said that if I wanted to go to work he had no doubt that I could get some at Big Springs, as there was nearly always a demand for labourers round the yard or on some of the extra gangs that were working at various places on the road. I was glad to hear this, for being entirely without money I was anxious to earn some.

It was morning when we arrived at Big Springs, and I went at once to the yard boss asking him for a job, and he set me to work immediately, first sending me up to the house to get some breakfast. Here I found his wife, who was just clearing up the breakfast things, and did not seem very well pleased at seeing me. However, she gave me some frozen apple pie and cold coffee; with this I had to be content. I stayed here in all three days, but the boss was such a cross-grained fellow that no one could do anything to suit him, and his wife was just a good match for him, being as sour as her own apple pie, and that was about the vilest stuff I ever put inside my lips. She used to call us railroad dogs, and on the smallest provocation abuse us individually and collectively, as if we had been a gang of robbers. I found my position here quite unbearable, so on the fourth morning, instead of going to work, I took the road for it, and started for Colorado City, which was distant about 40 miles. This was one of the hardest walks I ever had. I had had breakfast, such as it was, before I started. I do not know whether there are any now, but at the time I undertook to do this walk there was no station between Big Springs and Colorado City. I walked along the track on the ties or beside it, and hardly stopped the whole of the day. The prairie alongside, and as far as I could see, was rolling, but here and there it was broken with small streams, or little dry cañons. The only trees were mesquite bushes. It was in some ways fortunate that it was cold, for had it been hot I might have found the smell of dead cows and bullocks intolerable. These were lying in the ditch alongside the track; they had been thrown off and killed by the locomotives, and were rotten, swelled up hideously in the sun. I walked on all day, taking very little rest. The only living things that I saw were innumerable prairie dogs in their towns.

They sat on the top of their houses, on the mound made of the thrown-up earth from the burrows and chattered at me like a lot of monkeys until I was quite close to them, when they would suddenly disappear, diving into their holes like lightning to make their appearance again like a jack-in-the-box as I passed.*

Once or twice the east or west bound mails passed me, and I wished I was on board the one going my way, but I only saw one tramp who was going the same way as myself. Sometimes I might have been glad of a man's company, and if this wretched fellow had been clean I might have made a partner of him for a time. But he was so filthy and so frank about his undesirable condition that I did not care for him to accompany me. So I left him behind about sunset, and went on walking till it got bitterly cold. Presently I thought I would camp and try to get a bit of sleep for an hour or two. I hunted up some dead mesquite wood, which makes a good fire, and lay down close to it, falling asleep very quickly. 1 did not do much more than that, for I soon woke up and found that I had rolled so close to my fire that I had burnt a couple of holes in my coat, which had plenty of holes already. I got up and started out again in the black dark, for it was well on in the night now. The solitude was complete, so much so indeed as to

---

* Note A.—See Appendix, "Texas Animals."

be quite oppressive. Knowing that there was no town before I got to Colorado City, and feeling very hungry and tired, I kept pushing on in hopes of coming to it. However, I walked all night and it was sunrise in the morning before I arrived. As may be well imagined, I was pretty tired and hungry by this time, having been walking about 24 hours at a stretch without anything to eat. I was faint with hunger and utterly worn out, and as I had no money I was in a rather hard fix. The first thing to be done was to get something to eat, but how to go about it I did not know without begging it, and that was altogether against my religion.

As I was walking round the town, and about as low in spirits as a man well could be, I saw a woman with an axe chopping some wood. Thinking this was a good opportunity to get some breakfast without begging it, I went up to her and said I would chop her up a good pile of wood if she would give me something to eat. She at once agreed, and giving me the axe went into the house. She did not let me chop more than a few pieces before she called me in and gave me a good breakfast.

I shall have occasion to speak of this woman again, but here I will mention that she was the kindest-hearted woman I think I ever met, and she was a friend to me at a time when I was badly in need of one. Her husband also was one of the most sterling good-hearted men I ever knew, and I was in his employ afterwards for some time. His name was Pike; by profession he was a gambler and owned a beer saloon in the town.

After I had eaten my breakfast I went out and chopped some more wood, and while I was at it Mr. Pike came home and told me to come up town with him and he would see if he could help me to find a job. He introduced me to a butcher, who said that he knew a man who would give me work.

As we were talking, this very man, Butler, came down the street, and, on being told that I was looking for work, he said, if I would come up to his house the next morning, he would give me a job. Pike took me home with him for dinner, and his wife made me up a bed in the kitchen for that night. I went to Butler's as arranged the next morning, and he put me to chopping wood, a large pile of which he had in his yard. I went in big licks, and, although it was a good-sized pile, I chopped it all up before he got back at night. He was so pleased at the day's work I had done, that he at once offered to engage me by the month if I wanted to stay. I was very glad of the chance, as I wished to settle myself in some place, so that I could let my brother know where to find me. So I closed at once with his offer, which was $18 a month and board. This was rather low wages for this part of the country, but he said, if on further acquaintance I proved to be worth it, he would give me more. I now was put at a kind of work that I had never been at before. This was going round the town with loads of wood selling it. I used to hitch up a team and go out on the prairie and pick up mesquite wood one day, and the next I took it round the town and tried to sell it; if I did not get it off my hands that day, I took it home and unloaded it, and went out for more the next. A few days after I came here to work Butler hired another man, whom he kept chopping up the wood that I brought in; and some days I would take a load of this stuff out and try to sell it. At this business I was very successful, selling, I think, more than any other man in the town.

Butler was a kind of a jack-of-all-trades; by trade he was a machinist, and he had bought the exclusive right to sell and set up a kind of patent windmill pump in Texas; he also had a black-smith's shop, where he employed two or three men in shoeing horses, repairing waggons, and general blacksmith's business. Besides these, there was myself and the other man, who together looked after the horses and ran the wood yard. I was now fairly settled, and becoming quite a respectable member of society. There was a man named Fee working here also, who did all the carpenter work, for, although not a carpenter by trade, he was very skilful at the business. He always went by the name of Captain Fee, as he had been a captain in the Federal army during the rebellion, and had fought right through the war. He was a man of fairly good education and good common sense when he was sober, which, I am bound to say, was not on all occasions, for taking an occasional overdose of Bourbon was his one particular failing. He had a keen sense of humour, and one day he pointed out to me a man who was very flashily dressed, and had the appearance of being a " drummer," as they term a commercial traveller out there. Any person of judgment would have set him down as a howling cad at first sight, and they would have been right. " That man," said he, "took me on one side the other day, and, in a confidential manner, said, ' Look here, old man, I am a perfect gentleman, you know, but you need not mention it to anyone.' " Fee remarked that he need not be uneasy thinking that it would become generally known, as no one would be likely to find it out if he did not tell them. He remarked to me that the fellow was so dense that he did not see what was meant.

After being at this job for some time, Mr. Butler one day said I need not take the team out that day, but I was to come up to the shop with him, as he required me at some other job. This proved to be the sending down of a windmill that pumped the water for a livery stable. At this job there was a good deal of climbing and work with ropes. Of course I was right at home at this kind of thing, being a sailor, and Butler was so struck with my handiness that, after the job was done, he said to me, " You will be more useful to me at this work than at what you are doing at present, so, if you do not mind the change, I will keep you in the shop for the future, but I shall give you two dollars and a quarter a day, and you can board where you like in town." This was quite a rise in the world to me, as I boarded for $5 a week, which left me $10 a week clear. I had, however, to buy some new clothes, which were very dear in this place, so that as yet I could get no chance of saving anything. In fact, I never thought about it; I was glad enough to be simply earning a living after the hard time I had been having before I came to Colorado City.

The work I was now at, although it paid me better, was not so much to my fancy as what I had been doing before, as I am very fond of horses, and never better pleased than when I am working amongst them, After a while I got very tired of being in the shop, where I was most of my time working at the drill bench or striking for some of the smiths, so when Pike one day offered to give me the job of looking after his beer saloon, I accepted his offer and left Butler's employ. When I settled up I had just five dollars to the good, besides the new clothes I had bought. During the time that I worked for Pike I boarded at his house, as the saloon was a mere wooden shanty. It had been built outside the city limits. so that in case of any row or other irregularity the city authorities would not be able to do anything in the matter.

The place was very quiet indeed while I was there, sometimes a whole day passed without one customer making his appearance.

Pike was making some alterations and improvements to the place, and fencing it in while I was there, and at this work I assisted, in fact that was chiefly what I did, as Pike himself was there most of the time, and when there was any " beer slinging " to do he mostly did it himself.

This trade or profession of gambling, of which Pike was certainly a very favourable specimen, is not held in altogether such abhorrence or disfavour as some respectable English people might think. Of course I was pretty low down even in the social scale of a western town, but certainly among the working men we looked on " square " gamblers as rather " high toned " than otherwise. The fact that gamblers flourish in flourishing times, and that they do well when money is plentiful, made us regard them with some favour. They were a good sign, and the gambling that was done in Colorado City was a good deal at times. Every saloon had a gambling room, where poker, stud-horse poker, faro, monte, keno, and a wheel of fortune were usually hard at it. Pike used to play in the Green Front Saloon, usually at faro. I daresay some of the folks who disapproved of his profession would have liked to run him and his friends out of the town, but it would have taken some one with a good deal of courage to handle this lithe, long-haired Georgian, who was as gritty as a grindstone and as hard as a keg of nails. I liked him and he was kind to me, and I don't care in the least what he did for a living. One day up at his saloon he had a carpenter, lately from the east, doing some work there. This man was not doing it to please Pike, and on being remonstrated with he said "I'm doing this job, don't you interfere." Pike looked at him. "I tell you what, my friend, you may be doing it," said he, "but I'm paying for it, and if you talk to me like that, I'll blow a hole through you that a rat could crawl through. You mind me." And that carpenter did. I own I should have been sorry to have anything like real trouble with him. While I was at this saloon I got a letter from my brother, saying that he had made his final preparations to come out, and that he would arrive in about two weeks. Now, although my health had been remarkably good all the time I had been in the States in spite of the tough racket I had had, I now began to get a shortness of breath and a general feeling that I was fit for nothing. I also had frequent fits of vomiting and dizziness, but as I never had been seriously ill, I thought it would go away, and so I did not see a doctor. I kept on hoping I should again get well, and for a short time did get a little better. I left a letter at the post office, directing my brother where to come and find me, and one morning as I was standing outside the saloon I saw a man coming across the prairie. I recognised him by his walk as my brother, otherwise I should scarcely have known him. I certainly must say that for a man who was just fresh from London, and who, as I remembered him two years before was rather a fastidious kind of fellow about his personal appearance, he displayed a most extraordinary aptitude for converting himself into a most disreputable-looking ruffian in an amazingly short period of time. Rough as I was—and I certainly was rough—I was rather ashamed of the appearance he presented, and told him so, at which he laughed and said when he got his baggage from the depôt he would see what he could do to improve it.

Mr. and Mrs. Pike behaved in a very friendly and hospitable manner to him, and in a way that proved their goodness of heart, did all that lay in their power to make both him and myself feel at home.

My brother would not hear of my staying in town, though if he had wished to I have no doubt that he could have procured some kind of quill driving job, as he was used to that kind of work, but he said it was with the idea of leaving all that kind of thing behind that he had come from England. It being now early summer, or at least well on in the spring, the lambing time was in full swing, so of course there was any amount of demand for shepherds. I was at this time really ill, but did not think it was anything serious, so when my brother went and saw a sheep man named Jones, who wanted to hire two men as shepherds during the lambing season, I agreed to go with him, although I was certainly so ill that I had no business to leave town; and I very soon repented of having done so.

CHAPTER X.

Alkali Water and " 90 Days."

The sheep ranch to which my brother and I were going was out in Scurry county some forty miles to the north of Colorado City across the prairie. The day after we had agreed to go, Jones, our boss, was on hand with his waggon and a span of mules, by name Punch and Judy. We made a start rather late in the day as we could not make the whole distance in one day. Jones said it would be as well to divide the journey into two portions so that we should arrive at the ranch on the following evening.

That night we camped about fifteen miles from Colorado City and slept under the waggons on the open prairie by the track which was called a road. The following night we reached the ranch, unloaded the waggon, turned the mules out to grass, and made our supper of pretty bad bacon and coffee, which are the staple articles of diet in Texas. We slept in the house on the floor, though in a few days we should have to camp by the sheep corrals about half a mile away.

All this time I did my best to do my share of the work, but in reality I was a great deal too ill to be of as much use as I ought to have been, and when I turned out in the early morning I felt fitter to be in a hospital than to take a hand in any kind of labour.

Jones and a young fellow whom he had staying at the ranch looking after things while he was in town, went out to look after the sheep part of the business, leaving my brother and myself to catch the mules and hitch them up, and go for a load of firewood, for the lambing had not yet really began. I was now absolutely useless and my brother had to do all the work. I am afraid, too, that my condition had the effect of making me very ill-tempered, so that I said things that must have tried his patience very much, though he did not say anything about it.

We got back with our load about noon. After having dinner we went out about the sheep work; this was work about which I knew nothing at all. My brother had had a good deal of experience of sheep out in New South Wales, where he had spent some years, during most of which time he was employed in some department or other of the sheep business, having worked on many of the largest sheep runs of the colony. But I was as green as grass at it, and it fairly beat me. Jones gave me a bunch of sheep to take to a corral some distance away; this bunch consisted of ewes and lambs, and although the distance I had to take them was less than a mile, I do not think I should ever have got them there if my brother had not come along with another bunch, and putting his with mine we drove them together. Although the country here has no considerable hills about it, yet it is very rough and broken, the creeks in some places being bordered with bluffs, which though not very high are very steep and in many places quite inaccessible to horses.

The sheep seem to know instinctively where all the worst holes and corners are to be found, and when it comes time to corral them, they always scoot off and get into the worst places they can find. Some of the ewes will insist on disowning their lambs and running all over the country to look for them when they are in the bunch all the time. As the sheep men in Texas do not use dogs the work is enough to drive an ordinary man wild, and I, not being used to the job, and being unwell to boot, was in about two hours as near crazy as I ever was in my life.

Where the prairie is not broken up by small cañons and bluffs it is what is called rolling prairie, that is, the ground is undulating and it is not possible to see any great distance; it was in this kind of country where my brother joined his bunch with mine. He hove in sight over the top of a small hillock which had prevented me from seeing him before, although he must have been quite near me for some time. There was one ewe in my bunch that was a particularly bad beast; if she had been

my property she would undoubtedly have fallen a
victim to my indignation and her own confounded
stupidity. She had disowned her lamb, and although
the poor little beast was running after her bleating
pitifully, she would have nothing to do with it,
turning round whenever it came near her, and
butting it savagely, and making the poor little
weak-legged beast roll over and over on the prairie
like a football; I wonder she did not break its ribs.
This contrary beast would run wildly out on the
prairie to look for her lamb, and when, after a
considerable amount of running, I succeeded in
turning her back again, she would coolly walk
through the mob and out on the other side to give
me the same job over again. This game had been
going on for some time when my brother joined me.
Just as he came up what small stock of patience I
had was about exhausted. I had driven the
refractory devil of a sheep into the mob from
about all the points of the compass, and she had
just scooted off again. I was about done up with
fatigue and sat down on a rock to curse everything
in the world, but more especially sheep and lambs,
although I did not forget my brother for bringing
me out to such a job. When he came within
speaking distance he asked me what was the
matter. "Matter enough," said I, " these infernal
sheep are possessed with a legion of devils, I
believe, and I don't thank you very much for
steering me up against such a job, and I do not

know what you did it for unless you wished to qualify me for a berth in an insane asylum, for that is where I shall certainly go if I stay here very long." "You are ill," said he, "but never mind I will give you a hand and when you are better you won't mind it so much, though sheep are annoying beasts to handle at any time."*

It was rather late that night before all the sheep were corralled and we could get our supper, which by the way was poor enough, consisting of black beans and pork with coffee.

This was my first and last day's work here, for I got so much worse that I was not able to leave the camp the next day. I lay here for a week, being quite unable to do any work. I was very miserable indeed, for I could not make out what was the matter with me. I felt as if I had steel bands round my chest, and sometimes for hours at a time I had to sit upright to breathe. My legs were swelled to twice their natural size and were very painful, the skin being quite tense and shiny.

Jones was very kind, doing all he could for me, which was not much. At last I had a talk with my brother, and we came to the conclusion that it would be best for me to go into town and get medical assistance, as instead of getting any better I was only getting worse.

According to this arrangement next morning Jones saddled up a horse, Rattler his name was,

---

* Note B.—*See* Appendix, "Sheep and Sheep-herding."

and I set off for a small town called Snyder, Jones sending a man with me to bring the horse back.

I had not a cent of money of my own, so my brother got an order from Jones for $10, which was all the money he had earned up to this time. He gave it to me, together with two silver dollars, which was all the money he had in the world.

It was early morning and the sun was just up when I set out after saying good-bye to my brother. It was a long "good-bye," for it was six years before I saw him again, and then we met in London. But many a time in those seven years that scene has come before my eyes, and I could see him as I saw him then as I turned to have a last look back as old Rattler gained the top of the bluff. He was standing at the gate of a corral, out of which he was turning the sheep. His picture as he stood there stays in my mind to this day, and I have only to shut my eyes and I can see it all as I saw it that morning.

I was very low-spirited indeed, for something seemed to tell me that we were parting for a long time, perhaps for ever. Getting to Snyder was hard work for me, for, though old Rattler was a smooth enough animal and as quiet as a dog, the least motion was painful to me in my condition.

During this ride, which lasted some hours on account of my not being able to go beyond a slow walk, I suffered severely, and was very thankful when it came to an end and I was able to get a rest.

Snyder was not a large place, it consisted in fact of five houses; three stood on one side and two on the other of the track, which was called a road, across the prairie. By some people that part of it which was included between the first and last house of Snyder was called a street. This town was in its usual lively condition when I arrived. There was a woman in a sun bonnet sitting in a rocking-chair on the verandah of one of the houses and two cow-boys were sitting on empty kegs in the saloon, chewing tobacco and engaged in the engrossing occupation of matching quarters for whiskey. These human beings and a yellow dog who lay stretched out in the middle of the street, and every little while snapped at a fly that settled on his nose, were the only living things to be seen in the place.

Getting off my horse and giving him in charge of the man who had accompanied me, I went over to the hotel and was informed that I must stay there that night as there was no waggon going to Colorado City till the following day. This was annoying, but no more than I had expected; in fact, I should scarcely have been surprised if I had been told that I should have to wait a week. Having, of course, nothing to do, I took up my quarters in a rocking-chair and dozed the time away.

In the course of the afternoon I was roused up by an altercation that was taking place between

the proprietor of the saloon and a seedy-looking
individual on horseback who, from his being
spoken of as " Doc.," I inferred was supposed to be
a doctor. He was demanding two dollars which he
said the saloon keeper owed him for some pills.
The saloon keeper, on his part, asserted that the
debt had been taken out twice over in whiskey, and
although he was willing to call it square, in reality
he ought to make a claim for the excess whiskey
consumed by the doctor on the strength of the
debt.

This same saloon keeper, who was a fine tall
dark-complexioned man, was something of a desperado in his way. At least, if he did not kill
people for amusement or just to keep his hand in,
he was not averse from trying to, or actually doing
it if any reasonable excuse offered. I heard that he
got into an altercation shortly after I left with a
neighbour in whose house he was playing poker,
and that this quarrel became serious. Fortunately
he had no arms about him. But he rushed over to
his house and brought out a 17-shot Winchester.
His opponent in the meantime got a shot gun and
filled his pocket with cartridges. He fired out of
the window at the saloon keeper, who was in the
road. But he had to take snap shots, as the other
was very quick, and kept boring holes through the
frame house every time he fancied he knew where-
abouts his friend was standing. But this time no
one was killed. Yet the man inside was hurt, for

L 2

the shot gun exploded and tore off part of his thumb. As the accident was accompanied by a yell, the other thought he had killed him. So he ran off, jumped on his horse, and rode down to Sweetwater, where he remained for a few days, until at last news reached him that he had made a mistake. He went back to Snyder, and next Sunday these two men, who had done their level best to kill each other, were as usual engaged in a friendly game of poker. My brother says that the only thing hurt in the shooting match was an old fowl who did not know enough to get out of the way of the shot gun.

Early the next morning after my arrival the waggon was ready, and I made a start for the city. This journey was very trying indeed, as there were no springs on the waggon, and the road in places was rather rough. Of course, to a person that was well there would have been no inconvenience, but as every jolt was painful to me, it made the journey very miserable, and I was heartily glad when it was over.

On arriving in Colorado City I went to the Lone Wolf Hotel, where I had been staying before I went out on the ranch. It was late in the day, and I was tired, as in my then state of health the least exertion was painful to me, and I had had rather a rough time of it since early morning, being jogged about so in that wretched waggon.

I had some supper and went to bed feeling very miserable indeed. The first thing I did next morning was to go to the store and cash the order for ten dollars which my brother had given me when I left the ranch. I then went and saw the doctor, who told me I had an attack of dropsy, but before I left the place another doctor came in on some business, and after having a look at me he said that I was suffering from a mild form of blood poisoning caused by drinking bad water. The fact of the matter is I had very little faith in either of them, as I believe that the majority of these western doctors are just apothecaries' assistants who have come west with the view of bettering their own condition by killing their fellow men, and really know as much about medicine as a hog does of harmony. However, when the second doctor had gone away, the one I had gone to consult turned to me and said, "It is no use for you to stay in this part of the country, as you will never get well here; neither I nor anyone else can cure you as long as you stay. The best thing you can do is to keep what money you may have in your pocket, and go east out of this as fast as you can travel. When you get where there is good water and fruit and vegetables to be had you will not need any medicine, you will get well without it." On the whole he was not a bad sort. Most of them would have kept me till I had no more money to give them. I went back to the boarding-house and lay for a bit thinking of what the doctor had told me.

I did not like to go as I wished to stay round where my brother was; however, several people told me that they had known cases like my own which had been cured by leaving the country, the general opinion being that it was a sickness caused by the alkali water of Texas. Thinking that it would be best to take the doctor's advice and go east, I wrote a letter to my brother acquainting him with my intentions, and dropping it into the letter-box, I went and settled up at the boarding house, and, after bidding farewell to the Pikes, was then ready for the road. I made up my mind to get away that night if possible. I was wretchedly weak and short-winded, only being able to walk a few yards at a time, having then to sit down and rest. My legs were terribly swollen and ached most horribly. This was not very good shape in which to travel. However, it was a case of "Root hog or die" and I had made up my mind to beat my way as far as Fort Worth, and then decide whether I should go north or south. I had brought a blanket from the ranch and should have liked to take it with me on my journey, but decided to leave it as I was scarcely able to carry myself, let alone any baggage. I went down to the depôt after dark, and catching an east-bound freight, managed to get into an empty box car. The exertion of climbing in caused me the most excruciating agony. But I was so far lucky

that none of the train-men troubled me, so that I
made the whole of the journey to Fort Worth
without getting out of the car. It was morning
when I arrived, and not having slept all night, I
was about done up.

I bought some oranges that I saw, and with a bit
of bread and a drink of water, made as good a
breakfast as I cared about. Going out of town a
little way I found a sheltered spot, so making
myself as comfortable as I could, I lay down and
went to sleep. It was nearly sundown when I
awakened. I felt better and rather hungry, so
striking out for town I bought some more oranges
and bread, had supper and started out to see what
train would be through Fort Worth that night
going my way, for by now I had made up my mind
to go north.

There was a mail going east some time during
the night, and I would have taken my chances on
that as far as Dallas if I had been well, but I did
not feel up to riding on the top of a Pullman sleeper
or underneath on the trucks, and that is about the
only way that a passenger train can be held for any
distance. I decided to take a freight for it. There
were two or three going east and one north. I got
put off two of the east-bound ones and at last got
away on the one going north on the Missouri
Pacific. They switched out the car that I was in
at a place called Denton, about half-way to Denison.
There were not many trains running on this line,

and as most of them passed in the daytime, it was rather a difficult matter to get away. I stayed here two days, and as there was quite a lot of wild raspberries about it did not cost me a great deal for food. On the morning of the third day I was very much better, the swelling and pain had nearly gone out of my legs, but I was still as weak as a rat, and had scarcely any wind at all.

About noon this day a train stopped at the depôt, and for the sum of a dollar the hind brakesman stowed me away in the tool box under the caboose, as they call the brake van. In this manner I arrived in Denison, having now only one dollar and fifty cents in my possession. Being sick and not fit for hard work, I was now worse off than I had ever been before. I made up my mind not to spend any of my money for lodging, but to save it all for food. This resolve made it necessary for me to hunt up a roost of some kind, for, though the weather was mild, it was often showery, and I needed some kind of shelter. After looking round for some time I found a deserted dug-out, not far from town, and in this place I used to sleep at nights. A dug-out is the name applied to a primitive kind of hut which is built half under ground. The man who intends to build a dug-out casts about him till he finds a suitable place. The place generally selected for the purpose is a sloping bank; into this bank a square hole is dug and lined with whatever the builder can command for the purpose, sometimes rough lumber is used, but more often small stakes are cut and driven into the floor all round, to keep the earth from falling down. The hole is then roofed over with poles, on which grass or brush is laid as a kind of thatch, this being generally covered with a layer of earth, with a hole left at one end for a chimney. The dug-out is then complete. It is, in a severe climate, about the warmest and best makeshift for a house which can be quickly devised.

In the daytime I rambled through the woods eating the wild fruit, and when I was tired I would sit or lie down under the shady trees. I was getting better and stronger every day, and I began to think I should soon be able to work again, when suddenly I was provided with a job in a manner I never dreamed of, and certainly did not wish for, that is to say, I was arrested as a vagrant. As the popular expression went, I got "vagged." I was taken to the lock-up and incarcerated in a beastly box about nine feet square. At one end was a kind of raised platform, on which there was a pile of frouzy blankets. This hole was filthy beyond description, and the smell of it was sickening. In this place I was kept all day till well on in the evening without anything to eat, when I was brought a meal of pork and beans and stale bread. Hungry as I was this feed was of such a character that I scarcely touched it. Next morning I was brought before an official whom they called the police judge, the same thing as we in England should call a magistrate. I was summarily sentenced by this gentleman to ninety days in the chain-gang. There was not the least show of justice in the whole business; I was not asked to give any account of myself nor allowed to say a word in my own defence, but was hustled back to gaol, and was decorated with the order of the ball and chain; that is to say, they rivetted a ring of iron round my left ankle to which was attached a chain about two feet long, carrying at the other end a piece of railroad metal weighing about twenty pounds. Whenever it was necessary for me to move about I had to pick up this piece of metal and carry it about with me.

There were eight men in the gang besides myself, most of whom, I have no doubt, richly deserved to be where they were, for a lower or more degraded set of ruffians I never set eyes on. There is a class of men in the United States who make tramping a business, and who never work from year's end to year's end, except when they happen to get collared and put in some chain-gang or other.* For these men the thing is good enough, and they deserve nothing better, but it is rather hard when a man, whose only crime is that he happens to be sick and out of luck, gets treated in the same manner. My evident distress at the position in which I found myself was a great source of amusement to my

* Note C.—*See* Appendix, "Tramps."

worthy companions, who were never tired of cutting jokes at my expense.

We were taken out every morning under an armed escort, and made to sweep the public streets; in the afternoon we usually chopped wood for the use of the gaol. Our escort consisted of two policemen, who carried double-barrelled shot-guns. If any one of the gang had attempted to make his escape, I have no doubt he would have been shot like a dog.

However, I was so disgusted with my position that I determined to risk anything to get away if I could see the least chance of doing so. The chance I was looking for came in my way on the morning of the sixth day. On this particular morning we were sweeping up the road close to the railroad. There was a freight making up in the yard, and strings of cars were being run up and down the track close to where we were working. A happy thought struck me. I watched a chance when our guards were not looking my way, and edging close up to the track, I threw my ball over the metal just as a string of cars was coming down towards me. The first wheel that struck the chain jumped and made a great noise, but in a twinkling it was in two pieces, and with a bound I was up between the two cars nearest to me. Pulling one of the end doors open, I jumped in, and fell down like a log, and lay trembling for fear I should be missed before the train got away, and searched for, in which case I must have been found. However, in a few minutes, which seemed an age to me, the engineer whistled the brakes off, and I could tell by our regular motion that we were fairly off. As soon as I had assured myself that we were out of town I pulled the door open a bit to give me light, and then proceeded to dispose of what remained on my leg of the chain. I could not get it off as I had no tools, so tearing a strip off an old bandana which my brother had given me (he had bought it when working in Hull docks), I made one end of it fast to the end link of the fragment of chain, and pulling it up inside the leg of my trousers, I made it fast round my waist. Though I was not rid of it, this was a very good way of hiding it, though it was very uncomfortable. A small place called Colbert was the first place the train stopped at; in fact, this is the first stop north of Denison. It is two or three miles north of the Red River of the south, which marks the boundary of the Indian Territory at this part. Being anxious to get rid of the chain as quickly as possible I got off here, being pretty sure that no trouble would be taken to follow me when it was found that I had got clear away. I walked up the track for some little distance, when I came to a section gang at work. I had a good look at them, and coming to the conclusion that the boss looked a nice sort of fellow I went up to him and asked if he wanted any men. He said no, he did not; but if I was hungry I

could go with the gang, and have dinner when
they went.

Seeing that I had not misjudged my man I told
him the fix I was in, and asked if he would lend
me a file, "Certainly," said he, "come with me to
the tool-house, and we will soon fix that all right."
So I went with him, and, getting a file, with a few
rubs he cut the clinch off the rivet, and, taking a
hammer and punch, knocked it out, and the ring
fell off. I was now clear of all but the memory of
the chain-gang, and was very well pleased to be so.
As my health was now pretty well restored, I set
about looking for a job, but it was uphill work, as
all the farmers had their summer help hired, and
would not want anyone till the haying commenced,
which would not be for some time yet. The people
were all partly Indians here, although it could not
be detected in a great many of them, as the amount
of Indian blood was so small as to make no difference
in their appearance. During the remainder of that
day I was at six or seven different men, and came at
last to the conclusion that it was not much good
looking for any work in that part of the country.
I was walking away from an old farmer whom I
had been asking for a job when I heard someone
shouting, and, looking back, I saw young fellow in
the regular western cow-boy rig, beckoning to me.
I went back, and asked him what he wanted.
"Can you cook?" said he. I told him I never
had done any of it, but would try.

"Well," said he, "there is not much to cook; you
can fry bacon and boil coffee, I suppose?" I said
"yes," I thought I could manage that. "All
right," said he, "you will do, and what you do not
know we can teach you." He then explained that
he belonged to a horse "outfit" that was travelling
north, and he had been deputed to hire a cook if he
could get one to go for $20 a month and his board.
The "outfit" consisted of Bob Wilson and his
brother Jack, who owned the horses, of which there
were 500, mostly mares with foals running with
them. The man who had hired me, and whose
name was John Jefferson Baxter, and a half-breed
Indian, who went by the name of Chickasaw
Charley, and myself, making in all five men,
completed the crowd. It was now late in the day,
and as Baxter had got what he wanted, he led the
way and we went down to the camp, which was
situated on the bank of a creek close to, though
hidden from view by a belt of timber. As soon as
I arrived I was at once introduced to my duties,
and requested to cook supper.

Soda bread was one thing that I was told I
should have to make, and the materials being given
to me I was left alone. Now, I knew about as
much about making soda bread as the man in the
moon, and I don't know what sort of stuff I should
have produced if Baxter, who had been watching
me, had not come to the rescue, and showed me
how to set about it. It is very easy to make, and

after being shown once, I was able to get along all right.

Before we turned in the horses were all rounded up, and the saddle horses that were going to be used the next day were cut out and picketed with lariats so that there need be no delay in the morning. At this work I was quite new, but my companions were a hearty good-natured set of fellows, and though they laughed and joked at my blunders, did all they could to help me along and teach me what I did not know. John Jefferson Baxter was a type of the real thorough-bred western cow-boy, and deserves describing. In temper he was quiet and would molest no man, but there was a look in his steady grey eye that would at once have told a man of any judgment that he was not a person to be played with. By no means bloodthirsty, though he was always armed to the teeth, yet, if he had just occasion to do so, would not have hesitated a moment in killing a man. He stood about five feet five or six, and was broad for that height, and as wiry as a racehorse, with legs slightly bowed from continual riding. He was dressed in a buckskin shirt and leather breeches, with a broad-brimmed hat on his head and a large pair of Mexican spurs on his heels that clanged loudly at every step. Such was John Jefferson Baxter, and as good a specimen of his class as could be found in the western country.

CHAPTER XI.

On the Trail with Horses.

I was called up next morning before daylight to make breakfast. I was more at home at the job than I had been the night before, and acquitted myself in a very creditable manner. My work, when we were actually travelling, was to drive the waggon. So, after breakfast was over, the boys saddled their horses, I hitched up my team, and we started off for the first day's drive. We used to travel distances which depended to some extent on the location of good camping places, but the average day's work was from 15 to 20 miles, but sometimes a good deal less. To anyone unacquainted with the country, to drive a waggon and pair of horses would seem a very easy matter, but I soon found out it was by no means as simple a thing as I had at first imagined. In the first place the horses I had to drive were taken from the herd every day, and I seldom got the same team two days running.

The reason of this was that, being grass-fed horses, they were not fit for the work, and one day in the waggon was about all they could stand at a time. Not being a professional horsebreaker, this was rather rough on me, and sometimes I had a nice job with them. One of their favourite tricks was to turn sharp round and break the pole of the waggon, in which case I had to make another one, or to patch the old one up until I came where I could get one. A pole was an easy thing to replace if we were near any timber. All I had to do was to unhitch the horses and tie them up to the tail of the waggon, go off and hunt up a sapling that would suit my purpose, fell it, dress the branches off, and put it in. Sometimes, when I had a bad team, I had this job two or three times in one day.

On the waggon were carried all the goods belonging to the outfit, and a spare waggon-cloth which we used at night for a tent. I had an axe, an auger, a mattock and shovel, and these were the only tools that the outfit could boast. The mattock and shovel I found particularly useful in making roads, a job I often got, as in some places it was quite impossible to get a waggon along without patching up the road (or track, I should say, for road there was none). There are three big cattle trails that lead through the territory, called respec·tively the Chisholme, the Kit Carson, and the Great Western trail, but we were on none of these, as the boss thought we should get a better show for grass by keeping away from them.

Our first camp was near a place called Tishomingo. I heard it was quite a little town, but was not there to see. This was the first place that we camped for the night, but we stopped for a couple of hours in the middle of the day, and had some dinner.

Our first day's drive over, I began to feel quite at home with my new friends, and after the supper things were cleared up, and I had made all the necessary preparations for the following morning, we sat up some time round the camp fire and told yarns, they about western life, cattle herding, Indian fighting, and such things, and I about the great world which they had never seen, about my life in cities, and at sea. I think I astonished them more than they did me; in fact I believe they thought I was a very great liar, though they had too much politeness to say so.

One day was much like another, and we kept on north, following the east bank of the Washita river till we were nearly up to the south fork of the Canadian. When we got to this south fork we experienced our first check. The river was well up, though not in flood. The horses refused to take it, and we could neither drive nor coax them into it for a long time. It was about mid-day when we got there, and we did not get across that night : we tried all ways until it began to get dusk, and the boss then decided to let it stay over till the morning.

The next morning we got all ready and crossed with the waggon. We had to unload all things of

a nature likely to be damaged by water and carry
them over one at a time on horseback; for though
the river was fordable with care, the water came
over the waggon bed.

If the herd had consisted of horses, or if the
mares had not had foals running with them, I think
we should have got across without any trouble.
The mares, though knowing well enough that they
could get across all right, were afraid that their
foals would come to grief—at least, that is the
view I took of it. When the waggon and all the
gear had been safely conveyed across, we had
another try to get the horses over, and this time
succeeded.

I was on this occasion required to do a bit of
riding, being provided with a wicked little half-
broken broncho pony. This little beast had only
one redeeming point of character, and that was a
negative one. He did not buck. This was all the
fun in the world to the boys, so much so, indeed,
that after we had crossed the river, which we now
did without much trouble, Jack Wilson offered to
drive the waggon for a spell and let me ride, as he
said, so that I could have a chance of improving
my horsemanship; but, as I gravely suspected, so
that I might furnish diversion for the boys by my
lack of it. However this might have been, I was
glad of the chance, for I wanted to learn to ride
rough horses, and just then anything new was a
pleasure, even if I was not quite well. When Jack

gave me his horse first, we had something to do in
which my mount was as interested as anyone, and
though I found him hard enough to sit as he went
after the horses, who tried to double back on us,
that was nothing to what he did when he could
devote the whole of his attention to me. Perhaps
in some ways it would have been more satisfactory
to me if he had bucked me off at once and finished
the job, for at that time I had had no practice with
bucking horses, and must have come off. However,
he could not buck, but made up for it very well
indeed in other ways. Sometimes he stood on his
hind legs until I thought he was going to fall over
on me backwards; then he suddenly came down on
all fours and lashed out violently. Next moment he
threw up his head and nearly struck me in the face.
If he had done so he would have knocked me
insensible. Then he put his head down and kicked
like a cow, with one hind leg, and caught me a
crack on the heel, which made me glad that he was
not shod behind. Although he did not do it then,
more than once I saw him fairly stand on his
forelegs, and kick in this extraordinary way with
both hind ones. He broke Jack Wilson's spurs in
this way. Of course all the men expected me to
come off, but in this respect, at least, they were
disappointed, though I was often very near it; for
although the wicked little beast did his utmost to
shift me, I managed to frustrate his efforts. I soon
got very tired and sore, but I stuck to the job to

the end of the day, by which time I felt as if I had been kicked over every inch of my body, and when I dismounted I could scarcely move. Seeing that I was pretty well used up, Jack said I need not bother to do any cooking, as he would attend to that for this day. So I went and lay down and was very glad of the rest.

The next day I took my place on the waggon, and we proceeded as usual, camping early in the afternoon.

The weather, which had been up to this time fine, now began to get rainy, and things were not by any means so comfortable as they had been. On some occasions I had great difficulty in lighting a fire, and as the ground began to get soft and muddy, our progress was slow. On one occasion we had to stop for three hours, cutting brush to fill up mud holes before the waggon could be got over the bad place.

This kind of thing went on till we arrived at the north fork of the Canadian river, which we found in flood. It was coming down in a deep, swirling, ugly kind of a fashion, that at once made it apparent that there would be no chance of crossing it for some days at least, even if it started to go down at once. This being the case, there was nothing for it but to wait patiently till we could get over; so fixing the camp as comfortably as was possible, we prepared to put in the time as best we could.

The rain had ceased, and the sun was shining once more, so that we were as comfortable as is usual in this kind of life.

There being no work to do now but to herd the horses and see that none of them got away, all the boys began to turn out their stock of clothes, of which they all had about one change and no more. Soap was produced, and a general wash began. Jeff Baxter produced from some corner a shaving outfit and a pair of scissors, and informed the crowd that he was prepared to act barber to any one who required his services. I at once availed myself of them for my hair was long and ragged, and I had not shaved for a long time. After he had finished with me, and I had had a good wash, I presented quite an altered appearance, so much so indeed that Bob Wilson, who had been out with the horses, when he returned to the camp said, " Why you are quite a young fellow, I thought you were an old devil." We stayed in camp here for five days, by which time the river was down to its usual height, but on trying to make the horses take it, they refused again, and this time, do all we could, it was quite impossible to make them. After wasting a day in fruitless efforts to cross, Bob Wilson decided to proceed up stream to where there was another ford, which he said was a great deal easier to cross than this one. It was a long way out of our road or he would have gone there first. We started early next morning, and after a long day's journey arrived at the ford. Though it was dark, we decided to cross at once as there is always a chance of the river rising again, and it is as well to be on the right side. The crossing was affected this time, though not without trouble, as the horses evinced a most decided dislike to taking the water. The river was not at all deep here, so that it was not necessary to unload the waggon. The waggon team was quite played out this night, and the last part of the journey I had the greatest difficulty to get them along at all; in fact, when we got to the river they could go no further. So Jeff Baxter and Chickasaw Charley, who were riding fresh horses, made their lariats fast to the end of the waggon pole, and taking a turn on the horn of their saddles pulled horses, waggon, and all across, and we went into camp on the north bank.

The country to the north of the Canadian river is more open and less timbered than it is to the southward; in fact it is more like Kansas. Here we began to find a great difficulty in procuring fuel, sometimes having barely sufficient to do what little cooking was absolutely needful. Here, one day, I became aware that my companions were not what might be termed strictly honest. For some time a strange horse was seen on the outside of the herd, and Baxter said he thought that it was a wild horse, and belonged to no one. So when we went into camp that night they went out and caught him. He was a stud, and as fine a horse of his class as

I ever saw. After lassoing him, he gave a lot
of trouble before we finally succeeded in getting
him down, when it was discovered that he was
branded on the right shoulder. The proper thing
to have done in this case was to have let him go at
once. However, my friends did not think so, for,
seeing that the brand was somewhat similar to one
of our own, they at once proceeded to make up the
deficiency. I did not like the business, as altering
brands is felony; and, although I did not take an
active part in the business, if it had ever become
known I have no doubt I should have been considered an accessory, and suffered with the rest.

Their method of doing the business was ingenious
and effectual. By means of some small harness
rings and scraps of iron, heated, and applied over
a wet cloth, they managed to raise the flesh without
burning the hair, and so gave the brand an appearance of having been put on some time. This, of
course, disappears after a while, but would last
quite long enough to enable them to get clear
away with the horse if any questions had been
asked about it, which, however, there were not in
this instance. It soon became apparent that this
animal had been broken to the saddle, for after a
few days he became one of the quietest horses in the
herd, and could be caught with little difficulty at
any time.

A few days after this we had quite an exciting
time with a real wild horse. He was a bright

chestnut, and one of the finest-looking animals I
ever saw. One morning he came up to the herd on
a long swinging trot, his head thrown in the air, and
his long mane and tail floating out in the sunshine
like liquid gold. As he stopped short and snorted,
about a hundred yards away, he made as fine a picture
as well could be. He was a high-spirited fellow,
for he at once ran into the herd, and challenged
four stud-horses that belonged to us, but, to use a
popular western expression "they did not want any
of the pie," on seeing which he let go a few vicious
kicks at them and then proceeded to take charge of
the herd on his own account. Of course we could
not suffer that kind of thing, and so Bob Wilson
pulled out his revolver and was going to shoot him.
Baxter, however, asked him to stop a bit till he saw
if it was possible to catch him. After a little
trouble he succeeded in doing so by throwing his
lariat over his head. As soon as he felt that lariat
on his neck he sprang wildly away, and if Baxter
had been riding an ordinary horse, both horse and
man would certainly have had a roll on the prairie,
if no worse came of it. But the wiry little cow-
pony was well up to his work, and bracing himself
firmly he met the shock without a wink, and down
came the stranger with a crash, and rolled ignominiously on the prairie, where the little cow-pony
took good care to keep him, as every effort he made
to rise was baulked by the pony backing off and
keeping the lariat tight.

This fellow was so wild and vicious that it was not possible for us to keep him, as we could not spare the time to bother with him. When he was turned loose, however, he had the good sense to clear out and give no more trouble, by which piece of wisdom he certainly saved his life, as if he had stayed round he would have been shot without doubt.

The country was now mostly level prairie, dotted over in places by patches of small stunted timber. There were lots of small creeks to cross, and with some of them we had a great deal of trouble, not so much on account of the amount of water in them as the bad nature of the banks. One place in particular was very bad, the banks were very steep and muddy. Here we met with what might have been a serious accident. I was driving a pair of horses this day neither of which had ever been in harness before. I had had a good deal of trouble with them in the first part of the day, but they had been going very quietly for some time when we got to the bad crossing I am speaking of.

I managed to get them down the bank and over the creek, but going up the other side something frightened them and they swerved sharp round, overturning the waggon and all its contents into the creek. Luckily for me I fell clear of the whole affair. If I had fallen under it (and I really cannot say how it was that I did not) I could not have escaped being killed, for it took us all about a quarter of an hour before we got it righted again, as it had fallen in such an awkward position and the mud was so slippery as to afford no sure foothold. The pole was of course broken short off. The horses began to kick and plunge and gave us no end of trouble to unhitch them, but we managed at last to do so. There was not a great deal of water in the creek, which was lucky for us, as if there had been we should in all likelihood have lost a great part of our goods, if not all of them. As it was they were all wet and plastered with mud. This was quite bad enough, as it was late in the day and no chance to dry any blanket that night. Fortunately there was no scarcity of fuel just here, so making a good fire, we managed to dry some of our things, though the blankets were, of course, too wet to sleep in. However, we made out as well as we could without them, and were thankful that things were no worse.

Of course the duty of patching up the wreck devolved on me, so while the rest were drying their spare clothes (I had not got any to dry) I went out and cut a new pole for the waggon and put it in. After finishing this job I overhauled the harness and found several little things that had been broken, which in the confusion of the accident had not been noticed before.

The night being fine and fuel plentiful, as I have said, we did not put in a very bad night, as I made up a roaring good fire before I lay down to sleep and the night herders renewed it from time to time till I turned out in the morning to cook breakfast. We had no sugar to our coffee that morning, the sugar bag having come to grief in the accident the previous night; however, this was a small inconvenience and did not trouble any of us. After a day or two of travelling we came to the Cimarron river, or, as it is sometimes called, the Red Fork of the Arkinsaw. This is really the most dangerous river in the territory to cross, being full of quicksands.

Some few weeks before we arrived there there had been two bullock waggons swallowed up, the drivers barely escaping with their lives, but losing everything. The place we were to go over at was called " White's Crossing." It was necessary to exercise great caution to make the crossing successfully, so as to ensure the horses not stopping to drink. They were all watered before we got there, as if horses are thirsty no human power will prevent them from staying in a river, and if they had done so in this case it would most likely have meant the loss of a great number and perhaps all of them. They were also driven slowly to ensure their not being fatigued.

When we arrived at the river the horses were rounded up and two of the most trustworthy of the harness horses were cut out and put in the waggon. When we made a start the boss told me on no account to stop for anything till I got on dry land the other side.

With this last injunction he gave the signal to the other boys, and we started across, and owing to the careful manner in which the thing had been conducted we arrived at the other side without any accident. Our next camp was at a place called Red Fork; there was a store here but no village. Here we bought some things we were short of, and got the news, though the only piece of any importance related to a row that had taken place here some few days previous to our arrival between a man named Haughton and Chief Buffalo of the Cheyenne Indians. The row originated thus. Buffalo who was a turbulent mischievous fellow, had demanded of Haughton a toll of 15 ponies before allowing him to pass through his territory with his herd, which consisted of Mexican ponies or bronchos. Of course Haughton would not agree to this demand, and told Buffalo that though he had no right to any at all, he did not mind giving him two just to save a bother. At this Buffalo became violently abusive and ended by drawing his revolver and snapping it at Haughton, though fortunately it missed fire. This no doubt saved Haughton's life, as they were within two or three yards of each other. Haughton being a regular border man was of course well skilled in the use of a six-shooter, so without giving Buffalo the chance to fire again he drew his own weapon and shot him

dead on the spot. The few Indians who had been
with Buffalo, on seeing their leader killed, rode
away, but returned in a short time with all of the
tribe that they could muster up. This of course
Haughton had expected, and he had sent one of his
men down to a place not far from here called
Cantonment where some two or three troops of
U.S. cavalry were stationed to acquaint the
commanding officer with what had occurred and
ask for assistance. In the meantime he retired
with the rest of his men to the store, in which they
barricaded themselves. Before the soldiers put in
an appearance, however, the Indians had run all the
horses off, stolen all the saddles, blankets, harness,
provisions, and other property belonging to the
outfit, and building a large fire they put the
waggon on top of it and burned it up. After this
they retired, having done all the mischief they
could. When the troops arrived Haughton was
arrested and sent under escort to Medicine Lodge,
Kansas, where he would have to stand his trial for
murder. I have no doubt he was acquitted, but I
never heard how the affair ended.

We stayed in camp here for two days, during
which time we did some horse trading. Leaving
here, the country was very bare of fuel indeed, and
we had great trouble in securing enough to cook
with. The next river we came to was the Salt
Fork, which we crossed with no trouble, as there
was little water in it. The next few days' travel

were not marked by any incident worth mentioning, and in due course we arrived at Cottonwood Springs, which is situated just on the borders of Kansas, the camp taking its name from a spring of water and a single cotton-wood tree. It was just about a mile and a half distant from the town of Colwell in Kansas. Here it was the intention of Bob Wilson to make a stay of a week, and try to do some horse trading.

As the camp was to be occupied for some time it was resolved to make it as comfortable as possible. The morning after we went into camp here Bob Wilson started off to Colwell, as he said, on business, but in reality to go on a drunk. Before he went he left directions with one of the boys to ditch round the tent, so that in case of any heavy rain we should not have it running in on us. As soon as he was away, however, the man who was entrusted with this job, instead of doing it, just saddled up his horse and went to town on a drunk too; consequently the tent did not get ditched at all.

As luck would have it, the place in which the tent was pitched was a sort of dry gully, a very well-sheltered spot indeed in good weather, but a decidedly bad one in heavy rain, of which we had ample proof before we left it, though then the weather was fine and had been for some time. I was busy all day mending harness and setting things in order, and at nightfall the boss came back, and I could see at once that he was pretty full of liquor; however, he was quiet enough, and turned in without making any trouble, after giving the boys a bottle of whiskey which he had brought back with him, and which made them sleep very soundly. Some time during the early part of the night I was awakened by a clap of thunder, which was followed by rain-drops pattering on the tent. The rain kept on increasing, and in a very short time it was coming down in torrents. All at once I became aware of a damp feeling round my shoulders which soon changed to a decidedly wet one, and I made the discovery that I was lying in a small stream of running water. Just about this time the boss made the same discovery, and rising up with a roar he exclaimed: "Damn the man that ditched the tent!" This exclamation roused the rest. On each one discovering the position we were in he gave vent to some strong language, and all hands began to dress as best they could.

Everything was confusion and cursing; the stream steadily increased in volume, and we were fairly washed out of camp. Just as things were at their worst, down came a heavy gust of wind which laid the tent flat and sent us all sprawling and wallowing in the mud and water.

There was now nothing for it but for each man to grab what he could and make a bolt for the waggon, which was covered with a tilt. This was done, and in these most inconveniently close quarters we passed the rest of the night. Thinking to secure the best spot, I was the first in ; but before long I wished I was out again, for I was jammed up in a corner and could not move an inch. To improve matters I had something soft and slimy under my head, and could not make out what it was. In the morning, when we got out, I made the pleasant discovery that it was a smashed box of axle-grease, and that the back of my head and neck were plastered with the vile-smelling compound. This was my last night at Cottonwood Springs and also with the horse outfit. For some days I had made up my mind that at the first convenient opportunity I would leave, as at times there was some very shady business carried on, such as the brand-altering, which I already described. I did not like to be mixed up with this sort of thing, as it was sure, sooner or later, to end in disaster. Before leaving, however, I felled the cotton-wood from which the place takes its name, and chopped some of it up to make a fire at which I dried my clothes. I had been just a month at this job, and when I told Bob Wilson of my intention to leave, he at once paid me $20, the amount that was due to me.

After saying good-bye to my companions, who all wished me good luck, I left the camp and went over to Colwell, where the first thing I did was to write a letter to my brother, telling him where I was and that it was my intention to go north, giving him St. Paul, Minnesota, as an address.

CHAPTER XII.

Beef Slough and the Mississippi.

After leaving Bob Wilson's gang and their rather
shady proceedings I was once more entirely free.
Knowing that there was a chance of getting sent
out on a "labour pass" to almost any part of the
States from Kansas City in Missouri, I determined
to go there. Besides 1 heard there was a railroad
war on and cutting of rates.* This system of
labour passes is curious, and in the eastern part of
the States at times does away with the necessity
for "beating" the railroad. Labour agencies or
bureaus are to be found in most of the big cities
in the middle States, and I continually saw adver-
tisements for labourers for railroad work. All a
man has to do is to go in and offer to take the
job and pay a fee, which varies according to the
distance he goes. But it is rarely over $5, even for
more than 1,000 miles. He is then given a ticket
and is supposed to go to work when he reaches his
destination. Often, however, not one man out of
50 will be left when the place is reached, and if
any are left, they mostly want to go further. In
fact the system is a bad one for all but the men
and the agencies. I do not see that the railroads
get much out of it.

---

* Note D.—*See* Appendix, Railroad Wars.

I found on inquiry at Colwell that the fare to Kansas City was only $8, so for a change I detertimed to pay it instead of beating my way as I usually had to. This left me with $12 on which to accomplish the rest of my northward journey if I failed to get a labour pass in Kansas City. It was late in the afternoon when the train started, and I arrived at my destination early the next morning, which I discovered to be Sunday. For when I was on the trail we never knew one day from the other except by accident. Kansas City was not like some of the far western towns, and there seemed just then very little business going on. Its being Sunday was unfortunate for me, as it meant a whole day's expense and nothing to show for it. However, it could not be helped, so I just spent the day in looking round the city, which in many respects is very fine, as long, at any rate, as it is fair weather. Next morning I was out early and went to all the labour agencies in town, but could get nothing that I wanted. I could have got sent down to New Orleans and several other places south, but I got no offer the way I wanted to go. This being the case, there was nothing for it but to start out and beat my way there; so crossing the river I managed to jump a freight on the Kansas City, St. Jo and Council Bluffs railroad, and got up as far as St. Joseph that same night. For the next week I continued to go north with varied luck in the way of trains.

On waking up one morning after sleeping in a box-car at a place called Missouri Valley Junction, I found that my sleeping apartment had been shared with another man. He was a rather handsome young fellow and fairly well dressed, a somewhat unusual thing with people who sleep in box-cars. He was awake and sitting up examining his face and curling a rather fine moustache by the help of a small pocket looking-glass when I awoke. He was the first to speak, and he opened the conversation by remarking that I seemed to be in rather poor circumstances, which fact I of course assented to, as it was too obviously the case to make a denial any good, even if I had wished to make one. He then looked very hard at me and said : "Look here young fellow, if you are not too good to do a little crooked business I can put you in the way of living more comfortably than you seem to be doing at present." I asked him to explain what he meant by crooked business, for though I knew perfectly well what he meant, I wanted to draw him out and see what kind of proposal it was he meant to make. He then explained that he meant burglary and robbery of all and every kind that promised to be fairly remunerative; he also went on to explain what it was he wanted me to do. "I do not," said he, " want you to do any of the practical part of the business, for that needs a particular training and knowledge which you do not possess, and so you would be only in the way ;" but what I do want is a partner to go into the stores and offices and spot where the "box" is situated (he here explained that by box he meant the safe) and to take note how the windows and doors are fastened, and get a kind of a plan of the place in his head, as all such information is invaluable when the time comes for doing the job. As I let him run on and did not make any objection to what he was saying, he thought that I was quite ready to fall in with his offer of partnership; and when he put the question to me directly, and noticed that I hesitated, I noticed such a wicked look come into his face that I at once agreed to his proposal, intending to give him the slip that night.

Now that it was settled that I was to be his partner, he opened out in good shape, and told me he had served a term of five years in the Wisconsin State prison for blowing open a safe and decamping with the contents. He was a good hand at telling a story, and if he was not a very great liar indeed, must have been through a great many peculiar adventures. He explained to me that it would be necessary to do a bit of burglary on my account at once, so as to fit me out with some new clothes and a supply of money so that I should present a respectable enough appearance to make some excuse for getting into such offices and stores as my new friend had designs on. He showed me his outfit of tools, which he carried inside his coat, which was fitted with a lining of leather in which were a row

of beckets or small pockets in which he had stuck
all sorts of drills and jimmies, and other para-
phernalia of his profession. There was also a tube
and a small coil of blasting fuse and some powder
in a flask which he said were used in " doing up
a box " as he termed the operation of blowing
open a safe by means of gunpowder or some other
explosive. By this time I had made up my mind
that this man was rather a dangerous and undesirable acquaintance, so that very night I slipped
him while he was asleep, and got clear away.
When I was once more alone I jumped a " freight "
again and got up into the south part of Minnesota,
near a town called Easton.   Here I obtained
employment on a farm owned by a man named Cole.
I worked here for three weeks, during which time I
wrote to my brother, but received no answer, for, as
I afterwards found out, he never got my letters.   I
have worked for many different sorts of men in my
life, but I never came across such a beast of a
nigger driver as this fellow Cole; in fact, if I had
not been entirely without money, I would not have
worked for him a day.   I was ploughing corn, and
he would have me up at daybreak, and after I had
fed and harnessed my team, if there was five
minutes to spare before the breakfast was ready,
he would put me to saw wood with a bucksaw,
while he would stand and swear at his wife for
not having it ready. He used to allow the horses
an hour's spell at dinner time, but I only had half

an hour, and he would stand and watch the hands
of the clock, and the moment they were at the half
hour I had to be at something or other, either the
bucksaw again, or else he would have me take a
scythe and mow the weeds round the house. After
my day's work was over in the corn-field he would
get me in the barn on some pretence or other which
would end up in my having to turn the handle of
the fanning mill while he cleaned wheat to take to
the mill or else go to shucking corn till eight or
nine o'clock at night. He was a regular tyrant to
his poor little wife, and worked her just as hard as
he did me, and treated her a great deal worse than
I would have allowed him to treat me. For this,
as much as his conduct to myself, I very soon got
to hate the sight of him; for if there is one thing
that upsets my temper quicker than another it is to
see a woman ill-treated, especially if, as in this case,
she has done nothing in the world to deserve it.
After three weeks of this I could stand it no longer,
and told him so, but when we came to settle up he
tried to bluff me out of five dollars. I had engaged
for $20 a month, and having worked three weeks
I was, of course, entitled to $15, but he, for a long
time refused to give me more than $10. After a
lot of trouble, I managed to get another three out of
him, but do all I could he positively refused to come
down with the other $2. After a lot of talk about
it, seeing there was no chance of getting a proper
settlement out of him, as he evidently meant to

cheat me out of the $2, I lost patience, and picking up an old buggy neck yoke, I laid him out with it; I was in a passion, and hit him harder than I intended to. He lay where he fell, and turned quite white, so that I was scared, and for a moment I thought I had killed him. I went into the house, and making a bundle of what few things I had, I told his wife he was ill in the barn, and I guessed she had better go after him. However, by the time she had got out there, he had come to, and beyond a sore pate was not much the worse for the crack. When I came out with my bundle he was standing in the barn lot foaming with rage, and when I hove in sight he made a rush for me, but stepping to the wood pile I picked up the axe and told him that if he made it necessary for me to hit him again, not all the surgeons in the States would be able to patch him up. The fellow, who was really a coward, though nearly twice as big as myself, took water at once, and cursing and swearing most horribly he went into the house vowing he would have me arrested. However, though I stayed at Easton for two days, I never heard any more of it.

I still had the clothes on in which I had left Texas, and they were nearly in rags; my boots also wanted renewing, so although I had $13 I had to expend nearly all of it in getting some new things. The consequence was that I had not much left to travel with. Leaving Easton I started off to go to

St. Paul as I was sure that I should find a letter
there from my brother, and I also had an idea that
I would go out to Dakota in the fall and do some
harvesting and thrashing as I had done before
when I worked for Hank Beaver. But in the
meanwhile times were hard with me, for work was
very scarce, and with the exception of an odd job
here and there I got nothing to do. In fact it was
slow starvation. Some days I got something to eat
and others nothing at all. For the last five days
before I got to Minneapolis I had nothing but
some green corn which I picked in the fields as I
passed them. This was not very nourishing diet
and I was getting as weak as a rat.

As I was walking up one of the main streets in
Minneapolis, feeling, and no doubt looking, very
wretched, a man came out of a grain store and
asked me if I wanted work. I at once said yes,
though at the time I felt doubtful of my ability to
do it, as I knew how weak I was after the way I
had been living. However, I intended to try, as I
must do something or starve to death. He sent me
down to a warehouse from which he was taking a
quantity of bagged grain. My job was carrying
this stuff (maize it was) on my back from one end
of the warehouse to the other, a distance of about
40 yards. There was 120 lbs. in a bag and if I
had been in my usual condition the work would
have been quite easy to me, but in my then
condition of starvation it was as much as I could

do to stagger along under this weight. However there was nothing for it but to work till I could get the boss to give me some money. I told him I was so hungry that I could hardly work, and asked if he would give me some money to buy something to eat. He said he would see about it and then went away. I had been working about three hours and it was very near to dinner time, when I fainted, the first and only time in my life I ever did faint. The other men tried to bring me too, but as they could not they sent out for a doctor, and as soon as he saw me he said, as I was told afterwards, "This is a simple enough case, the man is starving, that is what is the matter with him." When the boss, who was really a good sort of fellow, heard about it, he was in a great state of mind, and said, "I did not think you were in that condition, why did you not tell me?" When I reminded him that I had told him, he said, "Oh, yes, but I had no idea you were as bad as that or I would not have let you work on any account till you were more fit." Of course, after this I got plenty of food, more a good deal than I wanted. I stayed for a few days and worked for this man, and he paid me every night. To save the expense of lodgings I used to sleep in a dry hole I found under a warehouse down by the river. Having now a couple of dollars in my pocket I stayed a day or two in Minneapolis to see if I could not obtain some job that would be permanent, but could find none. So I went to St. Paul, where I found a letter from my brother, in which he said he had come up to Chicago with some cattle from Colorado City but had gone back again, as he had been promised a job to bring some more up for the same man. As he said nothing definite about where or when I should be likely to meet him, and as I was offered work on a Mississippi steamboat, I determined to take the job and go down the river, trusting to luck to find some better job at some place or other.

I began now to care very little what became of me. I had been having such a hard time of it that I was nearly despairing of ever getting anything in the way of a decent employment. I only stayed on this boat until we got to the first landing. The name of the place was Redwing. I found that the work on board was much too heavy for me, and so I walked ashore. On talking to some men I saw on the landing stage, I was told that there was a place called Beef Slough, a few miles further down stream, just over the river from a place called Wabashaw, where the logs that came down the Chippewa River were rafted, and that anyone who went there could get a job at a dollar and a half a day and board. To Wabashaw I accordingly determined to go, and I set off and tramped it down there. Arriving at Wabashaw, I had to get across the river. There was a ferry, but the toll was 10 cents, and I had not got 10 cents to pay. This was a bit of a fix, for the river was too broad to swim and carry my

clothes across as well. I could certainly have
swum it easily enough without any clothes, but it
would be no good for me to be on the other side
with nothing on. I went to the ferryman and told
him if he would put me across that if I got work I
would pay him when I came back again, but the
old curmudgeon would hear of nothing of the kind,
at the same time remarking, in a significant manner,
that he had seen people like me before. From his
look and tone of voice, more than from what he
said, I inferred that he meant to be particularly
offensive ; so I walked away and left him.

But to Beef Slough I was going, whatever stood
in the way. On that point I had made up my
mind, so, walking back up the river for about a
mile, I looked about till I found a piece of plank
that was dry and would float. This was not difficult
to light on. There is always a lot of wood of all
sorts knocking about in this part of the country.
Having provided myself with a suitable piece, I
took off my clothes, made them up in a tight
bundle, and securing them on to my little raft, I
walked into the river, pushing it in front of me.
I was soon out of my depth and had to swim, but
the plank bore up my weight easily, and I just
went across at a long angle, drifting down with the
current. I made a landing about a hundred yards
below where the ferryman was with his boat. As
I dressed myself I could see he was looking at me,
but I would not speak to him, and, turning round,

walked off in the direction of Beef Slough, where I
arrived after about an hour's walk through the
woods. This path was very little used, as the usual
way of going to Beef Slough was by means of a
small steamboat that used to ply between Wabashaw
and there. But of this I knew nothing at the
time, or I might have saved myself the trouble of
swimming the river, as the captain of this boat was,
as I afterwards found out, a very good fellow, and
would put anyone who wanted to go to the Slough
across the river and accept his promise of payment
when he had earned it. The first thing that struck
me as I began to near the works was the number
of men I came across in the woods who were
comfortably snoozing upon mossy banks and under
the shady trees. I stopped and spoke to one of
these fellows, and asked him if there was no work
to be had at Beef Slough. " Yes, plenty," said he,
" for those who like to do it, but I am not on that
racket. I just sleep till the hash bell goes, and
then I go in and eat. Why," said he, as he raised
himself up, getting interested in his subject, " there
are dozens of men getting fat here, and never doing
any work at all. All you have to do is to put a
good ' front on,' and waltz in with the crowd ; no
one will know but what you are at work, and even
if they did, unless it was one of the bosses, they
would not say anything." " That is all right,"
said I, " as long as the fine weather lasts, but when
the winter comes on, how are you going to come

off then?" "Oh," said he, "I shall be in California
by then. I ain't going to stay this side of the
mountains to freeze to death in the winter."

Leaving this fellow to continue his rest till the
next meal time, I went on towards the works,
where I arrived in a few minutes. I at once went
to the office and asked for a job, and a clerk told
me to go down to the race and tell one of the
working bosses that I was sent down from the
office to get a job, which I did, and was at once
put to work pushing logs down a long channel with
a pike pole. This was the way in which the logs
were conveyed to the place where the rafters were
engaged in making the rafts up. This work is done
by men who are steadily at work at it all their
lives. They are "lumbermen," and can jump on
a log and push it about in any way they like, and
make it spin round under their feet, and, in fact,
are as much at home on a log floating about in the
water as anyone else is walking on dry land.

To make a rough guess, there were, I should say,
something like fifteen hundred men at work at this
place, and what number of different jobs there was
I am not able to say, but there were a good many.
There was a saw mill, a turning mill, and a black-
smith's shop, which gave employment to a good
number of men apart from those who were actually
engaged with the logs and the rafts. As soon as a
raft was completed, the crew of the steamboat that
was going to tow it down the river took charge of

it, and the Beef Slough people were finished with it. If the steamboat people broke the raft up as soon they took it in tow, they would have to fix it up themselves as best they could.

There was not house room for more than about half the men who were employed at this work, and the other half had to find a place to roost where they could. I was fortunate enough to secure a dry corner and a pile of straw in one of the barns.

The food was plentiful and of fairly good quality. The work was not hard and the pay a little over the average of wages for this time of the year. Taking all things into consideration, I began to think that I had at last struck a job at which I could stay and make a little stake and be fairly comfortable. However, I soon found out that the reason why the other things were so good was that fever and ague were rampant, and it was quite the exception for a man to stay here for more than a week or two without getting it—in fact, men were coming and going all the time, and few stayed for longer than a week, giving as their reason for leaving the sickness of the place and their fear of getting down with the fever. Seeing so many men getting sick and others leaving, I began to get scared, and after being here for a week, I took a notion to leave, and accordingly did so. There had been some lost time this week and I only had four dollars to take when I went for my money. However, four dollars and health was better than

forty and a dose of ague that would most likely last
me all the summer and perhaps kill me, deaths
from this cause being by no means an uncommon
thing.

Amongst the lumbermen who were at work at
this place were some queer characters. The following story was told me one evening of one old
fellow, who appeared to be a little cracked, but
who, if the story is true, must have had rather
more wit than some people gave him credit for.
He had been working in one of the logging camps
on the Chippewa River the previous winter, and
had provided himself with a good outfit of woollen
socks, but he found that when he happened to get
a pair wet and hung them up to dry, they were
invariably stolen. He used to growl and swear
and kick up a row about it, but could never discover the culprits. This kind of thing went on until
at last he came down to his last pair, and getting
them wet one day he hung them up by the stove to
dry and the next morning they were gone. He said
nothing, but on the following morning every man
in the camp on turning out found his boot tops cut
off. The man who lost the socks was in the same
fix as the rest. There was a general row, but as
every one had been served alike, it could not be
fixed on anyone in particular, though everyone, of
course, knew that the man who had lost the socks
had done it. For his part he looked on the scene
very quietly, and at last remarked, without a smile

on his face, " It 's an ill wind that blows no one any
good. I shall know now who stole the socks."

After leaving Beef Slough, I crossed the river
again to Wabashaw, and there I heard that things
were booming up at La Crosse and that there was
plenty of work to be got there. This town was in
Wisconsin, and I tramped nearly the whole of that
distance, getting only one lift of about ten miles in
the course of the journey. Ever since leaving Bob
Wilson's I had been going down hill and getting
more and more miserable. There, at least, I had
companions and plenty of food, even if I was still
in poor health. But things got blacker and blacker
to me, and although I never quite lost hope all the
time I was in the States, on this journey I came the
nearest to doing so. I walked along in a kind of
mist and took very little notice of anything, even
though it was fine weather. Perhaps if it had
rained I might have ended everything. I had not
the grit even to try and board a freight train. I
loafed along the road, tramping all the while,
trying, with no great persistence, to get work, and
starving in a kind of stupor. I suppose I was really
ill, for I have never felt like it before or since,
though I have often been in just as tight a place
when I was well and full of energy. All this
journey I had no blankets; even at Bob Wilson's
I slept in some belonging to the outfit, and now I
had to lie down on the ground, being glad if I came
across anything in the shape of shelter. And it is

not encouraging to a sick man to have to sleep in
heavy dew without anything but thin and wretched
clothes to keep any warmth in him. In this state I
at last came to La Crescent on the Iowa side of the
Mississippi River and opposite La Crosse. This
was a disappointing place; it was so sleepy and
there seemed nothing at all to do there. When I
arrived I had a look round, but as I could find
nothing in the shape of a mill or anything else
which promised work, I crossed over the river and
went into La Crosse. This was exactly the opposite
to the town I had just left, for it was very lively and
very busy, indeed, full of saw mills, planing mills,
and every kind of mill that is in any way connected
with the lumber industry. But although there was
plenty of work, there were also plenty of men to do
it, and I could not find any place that was short-
handed, though I got a promise of work in a few
days from one man. However, not being able to
subsist on promises, and being most extremely
hungry, I began to cast about for some means of
obtaining a dinner. I knew there were lots of cat-
fish in the river, for I had seen them, but the thing
was to catch one. I had no tackle nor the where-
withal to buy any. Certainly I had a nickel, or a
five-cent piece, but that was neither enough to buy
dinner with nor enough to buy fishing tackle to go
and fish for it. But fortune favoured me, and as
I was walking moodily along the river side, won-
dering if it would not be as well to give the fishes a

feed off my own carcase instead of trying to make one off theirs, I stumbled over the very thing I was wishing for, which was a fishing line—not a good one certainly, but good enough for what I wanted. There were no hooks on it, but I had my nickel and I went to a store and got two hooks. Being now equipped, I went down to the river, and having heard that cat fish were not at all particular in the matter of bait, I dug some worms, of which there were plenty to be had with little trouble.

Baiting my hook I threw it into a hole that promised well for a bite. However, after some minutes, feeling no pull I started to haul my line in, but found I was snagged. "My luck again," said I, "hooks and dinner gone at one fell swoop, and not a red cent to buy any more with." Hauling gently, however, first one way and then another, I felt the thing I had hooked first move and then come slowly away. So pulling gently for fear of snapping the line I at last landed it. When I got hold of the thing I found it was an old boot full of mud. Taking and washing it I found it was a right foot boot and in fairly good order, much better than mine was, so I tried it on and finding it was a good fit, I put it on and threw my own away. I fished for some time longer and at last I caught a good sized cat fish. There was no difficulty in cooking it as an old kerosine tin furnished a pot, and lighting a wood fire I soon had it boiling away in good style. Having no more money than my expended nickel I had to eat my fish without bread; however, I was too thankful at getting it at all to think much about that. After dinner I went down to the mills again but there was no chance of any work, so I lay round the water-side doing nothing but looking at the steam boats passing up and down the river and whatever else I could see to interest me. As night drew on I went to the mill where I had been promised work, and striking up an acquaintance with the fireman I got permission to sleep on a pile of sawdust in front of the furnaces. This fireman was English, and on my telling him I was an Englishman he became very friendly and gave me some of his own supper. The next morning I was down by the river side when a skiff pulled ashore from a raft-boat called the "Iowa" and asked if there was a man there who wanted some work. Although I knew nothing of rafting I jumped for the job at once. This raft was going down to a place called Dubuque in Iowa. These rafts are not really towed as most people understand towing, they are pushed down the river, the steamboat being behind or on the up river side of them. The raft is made in two parts which are lashed side by side, so that by casting them adrift and taking one half at a time the narrow parts of the river can be passed; it is also necessary to take them apart in going through the numerous bridges that span the upper river. The few days I was on this boat I was fairly comfortable and happy; it belonged to an old man and he had his wife and family on board with him. When we were going along all right, there was nothing to do, so we used to sit under the hurricane deck of the steamer and spin yarns. I very soon ingratiated myself with the other men by teaching them to splice rope, an art of which they knew nothing but which they were very anxious to learn. I was rather surprised to find that they could not splice, as there is a great deal of rope used about a raft which is continually being broken or "carried away," and great waste results from not having anyone there that can splice it. Sometimes when the raft got broken, as it often did, there was a nasty and (to me who was unacquainted with the work) dangerous job to mend it again. On one occasion, as we were passing near the bank in a narrow part of the river, by some accident either of steering or the current, one corner of the raft struck the bank. Of course the raft was at once broken and the way in which the logs began to slide and jam one over the other was enough to scare a man who was in any danger of getting a crack from any of them. I and one of the other men were on the raft at the time when this accident happened. I at once saw that it was no use for me to attempt to get back to the boat, as I had not yet learned to stand on a floating log, and the raft had lost its

usual firmness as the ropes that bound it together
were broken. Seeing how things stood I jumped
clean over the side and swam as far out of the
mess as I could get, which some of the older rafts-
men said was the wisest thing I could have done
under the circumstances. It took some hours to
repair this damage, but it was fixed at last and we
proceeded on our way once more. Everyone of
the river boats, whether raft boats or others, is
provided with an electric search light, and the
effect produced in some reaches when there are
five or six boats going down at night is very
striking. In some of the more intricate parts of
the river and when the river is foggy, of course the
boats have to bring up at night. We had to stop
one night on account of a kind of fly, it resembled
the common May fly very closely—if indeed it was
not that fly—the air was thick with them and they
clustered round the search light in such quantities
as to quite obscure it, and it was no use to brush
them off. I use the word quantities as numbers
does not express it properly, for in a few minutes
after they first made their appearance they could
have been swept up in bushels off the deck immediately under where the electric light was
situated, and they were trampled to death in
thousands on the deck till the planks were so
greasy everywhere as to make it impossible to walk
without falling, unless we all used the utmost
caution. It was like walking on ice.

On arriving at Dubuque the mate left, and the man who came in his place had some chum of his own that he wanted to give a job to, and so I had to leave. The captain told me that if I wished to go up to La Crosse again he would give me a passage, but as I saw nothing to be gained by going there, I thanked him for his offer and said I would stay where I was. My pay amounted to $4, of which I expended two at once in a new pair of shoes, which turned out a very bad investment, as they lasted me but a very little while. Still, I was fortunate at this place, for there was a steamboat here that had been laid up to get new boilers; she was just ready, and was going away next day. As I was standing on the bank looking at her, I noticed a man on board making a very clumsy attempt to splice an eye in a large new mooring rope. The mate, who was a fine big fellow, and a very handsome man as well, was standing looking at him, but evidently knew no more about the job than he did. My professional instincts were aroused at once, so going aboard, I walked up to them and said, "If you will allow me, I will show you how to do that job properly. I am a sailor, and understand that kind of work." The man who was at the job looked inquiringly at the mate, who said shortly, "Let him try." I took hold of the rope, and in a few minutes had put in a very creditable splice. This piece of work pleased the mate so much that he said, "I see you understand

your work, and we have no 'sailor-man,' so if you
want the job, you can have it." I thanked him,
and of course accepted it at once.

The term "sailor-man" may need a word of
explanation. On all these river boats most of
the men employed are what is termed roustabouts,
and are just ordinary labourers who are picked
up anywhere, and as often as not leave at the first
landing. These have no particular knowledge such
as is required of men who sail in ships. But, as
there is often some work to be done which requires
a small knowledge of sea craft, they always carry
one sailor who is called "the sailor-man," and who,
besides being paid $5 a month more than the rest,
enjoys certain privileges and immunities, foremost
amongst which is that, unless in a case of emergency, he is never called on to touch cargo; and,
even if he should be required to help stow it, he
does not go on shore and carry it aboard as the
roustabouts do.

The name of this boat was the " Libby Conger,"
and she belonged to the Diamond line of St. Louis.
The mate was a very nice man indeed, that is, to
me, although he used to hunt the roustabouts round
in good style; but that, of course, he had to do, or
he would have got no work out of them at all. It
requires a hard character to control the class of men
who work on these boats, as they are, as a rule, the
very scum of the country, and would not hesitate a
moment to take advantage of a man if they thought

it would be safe to try it on. During the time I was on this boat I was as comfortable as I could be in such a place, which is not saying much.

All the roustabouts had to sleep where they could find a roost, mostly amongst the cargo on the boiler deck; but I had a little place underneath the Texas, which is the name given to the pilot-house on these boats. It was merely a hole, to get into which I had to crawl on my hands and knees; but it was quiet and private, which was a great thing.

There were two men kept on regularly and called deck hands, whose duty was to see that the cargo was stowed properly, and when it was discharged to be there to see that the roustabouts only took the goods that were to be landed at that particular. place. Part of their duty was to " heave the lead," if we may call it so, when we were passing any shallow places. This operation was accomplished with a long pole, which was marked in spaces about a foot long, alternately red and white. I and these two men used to have our meals together apart from the rest of the crowd.

One day, as we were going down a broad straight reach in the river, and there was nothing to do, we were all sitting in the shade on the boiler-deck, when the conversation turned on working in the logging camps. One of the men, who had been engaged at this kind of work for some years, had some rather good stories to tell about what he had seen when he was up there.

" Yes," said he; " it is now some years ago—nine
or ten, perhaps—when bear was a great deal more
plentiful than it is now. I had been working all
winter in a camp well up towards the head of the
Chippewa River. The bears had evidently been
used to live in some of the cabins in the summer
season, when no one was ever up there except
now and then an occasional hunter; so when they
began to come out of their holes at the end of the
winter and early spring-time they often used to pay
us a visit, and they have been known to tackle
and kill men who happened to come on them
unarmed. Bears are mostly pretty harmless
animals in the summer and fall, if they are not
meddled with, but when they come out first thing
in the spring, lean and hungry, they are savage
enough. Well, one night when we—that is, myself
and two chums—had turned in, and had just put
the light out, we heard a shuffling noise outside
the door. Before we had made up our minds what
it was, something gave the door a bang and sent it
off the hinges and laid it in the middle of the floor,
letting in a stream of light, for the moon was at
the full. From my position in my bunk I could
see a large bear just in the doorway. He stalked
right into the cabin, and without paying any
attention to any of us proceeded to ransack the
place for something to eat. Fortunately for us we
were boarding ourselves, and had plenty of stores
in the hut; otherwise, if he had not been able to

find anything more to his taste, he would probably have turned his attention to one of us, which would have been awkward, as there was not a shooting-iron amongst the crowd. However, he reduced our store-locker to a complete wreck, eating what he wanted and spoiling the rest. We were obliged to lie quiet and watch the show until such time as Bruin saw fit to go, as we were quite without arms and so could do no more than resolve that his next visit should not be quite such a success, that is from his point of view. After getting all he wanted he went off and left us to clear the wreck and go to sleep if we could. Next morning I went over to another camp a few miles away to get the loan of some fire-arms, but all I could scrape up was an old muzzle-loading rifle. This was not a very good weapon, but better than none at all; so after loading it with powder and firing it off to make sure it was all right, I loaded with ball and put it in my bunk. As we had expected, as soon as the light was out and all quiet, the bear put in his appearance again. But we were ready up for him, and had made arrangements to conduct the show ourselves this time; so when Mr. Bruin was licking out the molasses keg that had been put there on purpose to attract him to a convenient part of the cabin, I leaned out of my bunk and, putting the muzzle of my rifle up against his head, shot him so dead that he never kicked."

During the whole of this trip the weather was beautiful, though at times rather too hot for comfort. The scenery on the river was pretty and varied. At one point there were some rather fine rapids, but they could be avoided by going through a short canal which had been constructed for the purpose. I was in hopes we should shoot them in the old-fashioned style, as many boats still do, for I rather wanted to see what it was like to shoot rapids in a steamboat. In this, however, I was destined to be disappointed, as we went through the canal.

We made a stay of some hours at Rock Island and then crossed over to the city of Devonport, which lies just over the river on the Iowa side. At this place we loaded a tremendous quantity of onions, both in barrels and bags. The levée was stacked up with the same article, and waggons could be seen in all directions loaded with it. One of the roustabouts, a mulatto, informed me that the place was called Onion City by steamboat men, on account of the quantities of this vegetable which were shipped from here. As we went on down the river, one day was like another in almost all respects, stopping here and there to pick up and put down cargo and passengers, and occasionally to " wood up," as taking in fuel was termed.

In due course we arrived at St. Louis, which was as far down the river as this boat went. Here I left her, having thought the matter over, and seeing that I was doing no good for myself—in fact, was going from bad to worse—so I determined to go to some point on the east coast and go to sea again. I took my pay, which amounted to $6, and went off to find out how I could best get down to the east coast.

CHAPTER XIII.

WASHINGTON AND "SHANGHAI."

THAT night I crossed the river to East St. Louis or, as it is sometimes called, Illinois City, but finding no train going my way, and being tired, I lay down on some bales of goods that stood on the steamboat leveé. Here I fell asleep and being very tired slept soundly—so soundly in fact that the mosquitoes which came out in full force later on had a regular picnic on me, so that when I awoke in the morning I was in a miserable condition, my face being so swollen that I could scarcely open my eyes.

From St. Louis east the whole country is a perfect network of railways, which, though their general direction is east and west, throw off branches in all directions. In consequence of this I was continually getting wrong as I tried to beat my way east, being carried out on these branch lines and having to walk back again; but after about a week of knocking about I arrived at Indianopolis after passing through Terra Haute and Greencastle, Indiana. From here I was more successful, getting as far as Columbus, Ohio, in one night. A day or two more of kicking about

brought me to Wheeling, Virginia, where I crossed
the Ohio River, and proceeded to Pittsburgh. I
was stuck at the Manongahela River, and as the old
humbug of a ferryman would not put me across, I
swam it. I dropped my clothes just before I landed
and got them all wet; indeed I nearly lost some of
them. My clothes being wet did not matter a
great deal as there was a hot sun shining, so by
wringing them out well and hanging them up I
soon had them dry enough to put on. At Pittsburg
I again crossed the Ohio, which, making a long
bend northward from Wheeling, and coming south
again, passes between Alleghany City and Pittsburgh at a small station just outside of Pittsburgh
on the Baltimore and Ohio railroad. I jumped on a
freight train and made my way to Cumberland,
Virginia, from which place I walked to Harper's
Ferry, the place so celebrated in the great war.
If I had not been hungry and footsore I should
no doubt have enjoyed the walk very well, for the
scenery was very fine indeed. The railroad bridge
crosses the Potomac River at Harper's Ferry, but
there is no footway across, consequently it is
impossible to get across without going in the train.
As I had no money it was not possible for me to
pay my fare, and as no freight trains stopped here
I did not see how I was to manage. I stayed there
for some hours looking for a chance to get over,
but could not get one; so at last in desperation I
determined to jump on the next coal train that

came by, as they slowed down on approaching the bridge, but were still going I should say 10 or 12 miles an hour. The undertaking was a dangerous one and meant certain death if it failed—death by being cut to pieces under the train. However, cross the river I must and would at any risk; so bracing myself up when the next train came I jumped, and managed to secure a footing on the iron frame, and held on by the top of the hopper which was higher than my head. These trucks are of a peculiar construction and made on purpose for the conveyance of coal; in shape they are like round hoppers and they are made of iron. I was in an awkward and dangerous position enough, for with my feet resting on a rim of iron about four inches in width, I was holding on to the rim of the hopper, the top of which overhung the base, so that nearly all my weight was on my arms. In this position I crossed the bridge, the Potomac River dashing and foaming along its rocky bed below me. To have lost my hold was certain destruction, as if I had escaped being cut to pieces by the train, the fall into the river would have been quite sufficient to kill me. The train pulled up at the other side of the river at a place called Sand Point, where I got off, very glad to be there to get off alive. The conductor came along and after calling me names for risking my life in that foolhardy fashion gave me half a dollar. I thanked him and said "if some one had given me this the other side of the river I need not have risked my life to cross it." It was now getting dark so I determined to go no further that night, and found a quiet corner to sleep in, in the round-house as they call the engine sheds. I was sleeping here most comfortably when an old cripple of a watchman came poking round, and finding me, turned me out. This was the first time I was ever turned out of a similar place, and I have often slept in them. Having to turn out of my shelter I went into a lumber yard and slept there for the rest of the night; it was not cold but I got wet through with the dew.

As soon as daylight came in I was up and started to walk east, along the towing-path of the Chesapeake and Ohio Canal. At a place called Point of Rocks I overtook a canal-boat that was going down to the city of Washington. The captain of this boat said that if I chose to take a spell of driving the mules I could go with them and have my food on the boat. This being a much more satisfactory way of travelling than tramping it and hunting for grub, I accepted his offer, and for a day or two became a mule driver. This canal follows the course of the Potomac River, and the scenery is very beautiful. I was very comfortable indeed, having a good pile of hay to sleep on at night, and as much to eat as I wanted. The captain of this boat had his wife with him and they were very nice kind people, the other two men who completed the crew of the barge were also good fellows in

their way, and I got on very well with them.
The canal comes to an end before Washington is
reached, and the boats are locked out into the river.
This is not done in the usual way by a succession
of levels, but the boat that is going out is put in
a large tank, which is then lowered down an inclined
plane to the level of the river. This place is constructed on the same principle as a slip for repairing
ships. The boat has then to be towed the
remainder of the distance by a steamer. When the
boat arrived at her discharging berth the captain
gave me a dollar, which was more than I expected,
as I had not stipulated for any wages and did not
expect any. Being now in a seaport I began to
look about for a ship, as I intended to go to sea
again; indeed there was not anything else I could
do as far as I could see. There were no ocean-going
ships here, so after a day's looking round I found
a schooner that was in want of a man, and after
some haggling as to wages, I agreed to go in her
for $25 a month, which sum the captain, who was
a regular skinflint, said was far too much. Her
cargo was all in and she was ready to go to sea,
Savannah, in the State of Georgia, being the port to
which she was bound. However, we never reached
Savannah, for after getting out of Chesapeake Bay,
as we were lying becalmed a distance of about
15 or 20 miles from the land, a steamboat that was
bound in ran us down. This occurred in the
middle watch, or between midnight and four in the

morning, and I was below at the time. However, hearing the shouts of those on deck, and feeling the impact, I at once suspected what was up, and running on deck in my shirt I saw that we were sinking fast. Not wishing to be sucked down with her, I ran along the deck to the taffrail and jumping overboard swam as far away as I could get. I was not many yards away, however, when she foundered; the suck of the water was very strong, and I could feel it pull me back like a strong current. The collision was caused entirely by our own carelessness, as there were no lights out, and I have every reason to believe that the captain, who was in charge of the deck, was asleep.

The steamboat people were, to do them justice, remarkably smart in getting a boat in the water and coming to our assistance, and it was owing to this promptitude on their part that no lives were lost. We were seven hands all told, that is, captain, mate, four able seamen, of which I was one, and a boy who was cook and steward, but we were all saved. This under the circumstances was little short of miraculous, as I was the only swimmer in the crowd. I shall not mention the names of these ships nor the persons concerned, as the captain of the schooner is possibly alive, and having made some damaging statements about him (which are, however, quite true), I do not wish to mention names for obvious reasons. The steamboat was bound up to Baltimore, where we were all landed next day. I could now pose as a shipwrecked sailor, though I was in reality little the worse for the misadventure, as I had had nothing to lose and not having any wages to take all that remained for me to do was to get another ship as soon as possible. In this destitute condition I met a man who was, I think, a minister of some sort or other, a few hours after I came on shore, and he was very kind to me. On my expressing a wish to go to New York he took me to the railroad depôt and bought me a ticket to that place and gave me a dollar into the bargain. It was early morning when I arrived in New York, and at once I went to work to find a ship. As I was walking about by the East River quays I was accosted by a man who turned out to be a boarding-house runner. I knew quite enough of this class of people to wish to keep clear of them, but my condition was so bad at that time that it really seemed as if it could not be any worse. As this man did not seem to be a very bad specimen of his class, and as he promised to get me a good job in a coaster, I went with him to the house he was running for, which was a low den situated in a street off the Bowery. I did not like the look of the place much, but I was as near as may be destitute, having spent twenty-five cents out of my dollar for some breakfast, so that any kind of shelter with the certainty of food of some sort was an improvement in my condition. I stayed at this place till late in the afternoon, when

the man who had brought me there in the morning
came in and told me that he had been out all day
trying to secure me a good job, and that he had at
last succeeded. He became very friendly and
talkative and ended by asking me to have a drink.
Not suspecting any foul play I agreed, and we went
up to the dirty bar and he ordered two glasses of
lager beer, one of which I drank and he the other.
I had not had this drink down many minutes
before I began to feel very queer, so much so that
I at once suspected that I had been drugged, which
was indeed the case for I was soon insensible.

When I regained consciousness I found myself in
a bunk in a place that I recognised as the
forecastle of a large ship. My head was as heavy
as lead and ached horribly, and altogether I felt
miserably ill; but I knew at once that I had been
the victim of a practice at one time very common
in all American ports, but now happily of much
rarer occurrence, that is known amongst seafaring
men as " Shanghai-ing." This is drugging men or
intimidating and conveying them on board of an
outward-bound ship against their will. The
boarding-house masters by the collusion of the
ship masters (most of whom are as big scoundrels
as the boarding masters, and some a great deal
worse), manage to net about three months of the
man's wages in advance.

I could tell by the steadiness of the ship and the
lack of all noise that the ship must be at anchor

somewhere or other, and as I could see no one awake, I determined, if possible, to circumvent the nice gang of scoundrels that had put me there, and get away even if I had to swim for it, as I expected I should. Getting out of the bunk, I crawled quietly upon deck. The night was dark, there being no moon, but the stars were out, and I could see the vessel's spars clearly against the sky, by which I made out she was a full-rigged ship, carrying three skysails. There were also boom irons aloft on her lower and topsail yards, which made it plain to me that she carried those sailors' pet abominations, known as stunsails. All these details I gathered at a single glance, for I was quite at home at this kind of thing, and made up my mind that I would not go to sea in her, if I had to commit murder to get away. As I formed this resolution, my hand, which was resting on the fore hatch, came in contact with something hard and cold, which, on closer inspection, turned out to be a large sailor's sheath knife. This weapon I at once secured, and crept into the shade of the bulwarks in the way of the fore rigging. From this position I had a clear view right aft to the break of the poop. There was a man pacing up and down the quarter-deck, one of the officers I judged he was, for in ships of this kind the anchor watch is rarely trusted to a sailor. I watched my opportunity, and putting my head over the rail, I surveyed my position, and found we were lying in the middle of the river, and the tide,

which was flood, was running very strong, so that
to attempt to swim ashore with my clothes on would
have been rather a risky piece of business. I must
find something or other to help me, but that fellow
on the quarter-deck would be sure to spot me if I
went rummaging round, and I knew enough of
what these ships are to know that I should either
have to kill him or be severely ill-used and put
under lock and key till the ship was out to sea. I
accordingly crept aft a foot or two at a time, till I
was in the main rigging, and just abreast of where
this man was walking up and down. He did not
notice me, and I rather fancy it was a lucky thing
for him that he did not, for I had the knife in my
hand that I had found on the fore hatch, and had
decided that if he attempted to interfere with me
to kill him at once, and then make a jump for it,
and risk whether I got ashore or drowned, rather
than make a passage in an American ship of that
class. However, there was no need to do so, as he
did not even look my way till I was past him, and in
the alley-way between the after-deck house and the
bulwarks. Here the darkness was complete, and I
was quite safe as long as I did not make noise
enough to attract anyone's attention who might
happen to be awake in the cabin. I crawled right
aft to the taffrail, and quietly put the end of the
spanker boom sheet over, and paid it out to the
pin. I then cut down one of the life-buoys, and,
slipping it over my arm, I grasped the rope and

lowered myself noiselessly into the water, and, letting go, I allowed the tide to take me about a hundred yards up the river, and then struck out for the shore.*

In about twenty minutes, during which time I had all my work to do, I reached, not the shore, but the off side of a Norwegian barque that was lying alongside one of the wharfs on the New York side. There was a side ladder over which I got hold of, and, letting the life-buoy go, I climbed on board. There was a watchman awake, and he could speak a little English. I told him I had fallen overboard from a ship in the river. He had a fire in the galley, and dried my clothes for me, and gave me some hot tea, for which I was very thankful. He let me turn in, in his own bunk, till next morning, when he gave me some breakfast, and I went to work to find a ship on my own account, deciding not to have anything more to do with crimps or such people. I should have liked to make a long voyage before going back to England, but could find no suitable vessel. At last, after tramping round all the quays, I came to the Anchor Line shed, by which was lying a steamboat belonging to that line, called the " Anchoria," and on going on board I found they were in want of a man. I asked the mate for the job, and he engaged me at once. The " Anchoria " was bound for Glasgow.

---

* NOTE F.—*See* Appendix, " American Shipmasters."

CHAPTER XIV.

THE NET RESULT.

IT was five days after I joined the "Anchoria" before she sailed. During this time I was engaged about the usual work that is carried on in a steamboat, and was as comfortable as could be expected, seeing that I had no clothes but just what I stood upright in, and consequently was unable to change when I got wet. These clothes, by the way, were of such a sort as deserves a little description. They consisted of a cotton shirt, a pair of coarse duck trousers much the worse for wear, which one of the sailors on the boat that took me to Baltimore had given me, a pair of old low shoes, no stockings or underclothes of any kind, and a felt hat, out of which the crown was fast disappearing. Of course I had no oilskins, so that when it rained I had to get wet; neither had I any blanket or bedding of any sort, and had to sleep on the bare bunk boards. But for this I cared little, as I was used to sleeping hard, and did not mind it much, although the month was October, and when we got to sea the weather was very cold. However, it never is very warm in the North Atlantic even in the summer time, at least I never found it so, and I have been across two or three times. The number of stowaways that were coming to light every day was, I thought, significant of the hard state of the times on the east coast at this period. They were turning up out of all sorts of holes and corners by twos and threes all the passage until they footed up a total of 17. As they were found they were marched aft to the bridge, where the captain or officer who was in charge at the time would ask them in a stern tone of voice what they were doing there, and what they meant by it, &c. Then, turning to the boatswain, he would say, "Bo'sun, put them to work," after which no more notice was taken of them, for they were all allowed to go their way when we arrived in Glasgow without any proceedings being taken against them.

Two sailors from the watch on deck used to go into the bunkers to help trim the coal down to the firemen, and this being a warm job the boatswain's mate used generally to send me down, as he knew I had no clothes in which to stand the weather. This, coupled with the fact that I used to sleep in a white-washed jib cover which the boatswain's yoeman lent me to use instead of a blanket, very soon made me present a curious chequered appearance; in fact, I was a regular study in black and white; but by rubbing in and blending it soon changed to grey, and from that, on account of the superior supply of coal-dust, to black, at which it remained for the rest of the passage. When we arrived in Glasgow it was raining heavily, and the town was enveloped in steaming fog, while under foot the mud was plentiful; in fact, a more dreary, miserable ending to a hard and, for the most part, miserable pilgrimage could scarcely be imagined; and, as a net result of my American travels, I was in possession of just 30s.

Before I finish I should like to say something in explanation of what will doubtless strike the ordinary reader as a very erratic and foolish series of nearly aimless wanderings. In the first place there is, I firmly believe, in every man a latent spirit of unrest which only requires a proper opportunity to manifest itself, and the more it is indulged the stronger it grows, until the habit of vagabondising is firmly established. Then there is the temptation in America to go West, the hope of getting something better, which often is really the throwing away of the substance to grasp at the shadow. When it is found to be a shadow, the deluded one turns away and consoles himself by grasping still another. So the thing goes on till at last, through wandering and hard knocks, the thin veneering of civilisation gets worn off and leaves little more than the native savage, who is quite satisfied as long as he gets sufficient food to keep him from starvation. I did not get quite so far as this, though I have seen many who did, men too of education and culture, who wandered from place to place, who rarely did any work, and having lost the last vestiges of self-respect, were not ashamed to beg everything that they needed. Even in these cases, except the very worst ones, there seems to be some hope, something to which they are journeying, something that shall alter their course of life and make them what they were, and restore to them what they have lost. It is ever near but never attained, and they go down to their nameless graves looking forward to something that in the very nature of things they can never obtain.

THE END.

APPENDIX.

Note A.—TEXAS ANIMALS, p. 146.

The fauna of Texas is very varied, and a naturalist may find plenty there for his note-book, and much to reflect on, if he be a contemplative man. A hunter may satisfy himself, too, if he goes into the extreme west and north-west, but he must be quick about it, for I received a letter the other day from a friend of mine in the south part of the Panhandle of Texas, in which he told me that all the land was getting fenced in, even in those parts that I knew in 1884 as wide and open prairie, and when fences come the beasts go, deer and antelope retreat, and panther and cougar are hunted and shot by those who own sheep, cattle, and horses. I am no naturalist, and no great hunter. At the risk of causing a smile of contempt, I must confess that I can hold a shot gun, a "double-pronged scatter gun," or a rifle in my hands without shooting at anything I see. I have let antelope and deer pass me without even letting the gun off, and have spared squirrels and birds innumerable that most of my friends would have promptly slain ; but I take great interest in animal life, and am fond of watching the denizens of prairie or forest.

When on my friend Jones's ranche· in 1884, I sometimes went wild turkey hunting or potting ; we used to choose a moonlight night and lie under the trees, where they roosted, and shoot them on the branches. It was mere butchery, and the sole excitement consisted in the doubt as to whether any of the big birds would come or not, and the chief interest to me was the conversation of my wild Texan friends, who were stranger than turkeys to me.

There were not many birds of prey around us, except the big slow-sailing turkey buzzards, which are protected by law as useful scavengers. Nevertheless, I shot at one once, and, having missed it, I never tried again.

My great friends were the hares or jack rabbits, which are fast, but very easy to shoot, for if I saw one coming my way loping or cantering along, I stood stock still, and he would come past me without taking the least notice of my presence, probably imagining I was only a curious-shaped stump. Sometimes I found them in the dry arroyos or watercourses, and threw stones at them. They rarely ran away at once at full speed, but for the most part went a little distance, and sat up to look at me, waiting for two or three stones, until they made up their minds that I was decidedly dangerous.

Another little animal was the cotton-tail rabbit, so called from the white patch of fur under the tail, which is as bright as cotton bursting from the pod. I killed one once more by impulse than anything else. It ran from under my feet when I had a knife in my hand. I threw it at the rabbit, and to my surprise knocked it over, for I am a very bad shot with that sort of missile.

The prairie dogs or marmots were in tens of thousands round us, and I used to amuse myself by shooting at one in particular with the rifle. His hole was 100 yards from our camp, and he would come out and sit on his hill every now and again, and then go nibbling round at the grass. I shot at him a dozen times, and once cut the ground under his belly, but never killed him. They are extremely hard to get even if shot, for they manage to run into their burrows somehow, even if mortally wounded. The Texans believe they go back even when quite dead; but then they are rather credulous, for some of them believe that the rattlesnake lives in friendly terms with the inmates of the burrows. The rattlesnakes were very numerous, for one day I killed seven. The first one I saw threw me into a curious instinctive state of fury, and I smashed it into pieces, trembling all over like a horse who has nearly stepped on a venomous snake. Those Texans who do not believe in the friendship of snake and prairie dog say that it is possible to make the rattler come out of a hole he has taken refuge in by rolling small pieces of dirt and earth down it. For they assert that the prairie dogs earth up the mouth of the burrow when they know a snake is in it, and the reptile knows what is about to happen.

Of other snakes, there were the mocassins, water snakes and esteemed very deadly. It is said that when an Indian is bitten by by one of these he lies down to die, without making any effort to save his life, whereas if a rattlesnake has harmed him, he usually cures himself. Besides these there were the omnipresent garter snakes, and the grey or silver coach whip, both harmless. The bull snake is said to grow to an enormous size, and is a kind of North American python or boa. About five miles from our camp was an old hut, which was occupied by a sheep-herder whom I knew. One night he heard a noise, and looking out of his bunk saw, by the dim light of the fire, an enormous snake crawling out of a hole in the corner of the room. He jumped out of bed and ran outside, and found a stick. He killed it, and it measured nearly 11 feet. It is called bull snake because it is popularly supposed to bellow, but I never heard it make any noise of such description.

On these prairies there are occasionally to be found cougars, commonly called panthers or "painters," although erroneously. In British Columbia they are called mountain lions, and the same name is applied to them in California, unless they are called California lions. I am informed by a naturalist friend that they are the same species as the South American puma. I knew a man in Colorado city who was a great hunter of these animals, and he had half a dozen hunting dogs torn and scratched all over their bodies, with ears missing, and one with half a tongue, who had suffered from the teeth and claws of these cougars. He kept one in a cage, which was much too small for it, and I was often tempted to poison it to put an end to its misery. This man had a regular menagerie at the back of his house, consisting of various birds, this cougar, and two bears.

These bears are not infrequently to be met with on the prairies, and, while I was staying in town one was brought in in a wagon. Bruin had been captured by four cowboys, who had lassoed and tied it. He weighed about 600 lbs., and was a black bear, for the cinnamon and grizzly do not, I believe, range in open level country.

Besides these harmful animals, there were plenty of antelope to be found, if one went to look for them, and the cowardly slinking coyote was often to be seen as one rode across the prairie; and often in walking I found tortoises, with bright red eyes. These were small, about 6 ins. long. In the creeks were plenty of mud turtles, which are fond of scrambling on to logs to sun themselves. If disturbed they drop into the water instantly, giving rise to a saying to express quickness, "like a mud turtle off a log."

I have said nothing of bison. Perhaps there are none now, but in 1884 there were supposed to be still a few on the Llano

Estacado or Stakes Plain. I knew one man who used to go hunting them every year and usually killed a few. But the last time I saw him he was on a "jamberee," or spree, and killed his unfortunate horse by tying it up without feeding it or giving it water, while he was drinking or drunk, and so he did not make his usual trip. But I imagine there can be few or none left now, and probably the only representatives of the race are in the National Park.

Note B.—SHEEP AND SHEEP-HERDING, p. 160.

With the introduction of fences, which are now coming in with tremendous rapidity, sheep herding as an art is inevitably doomed. When I knew north-west Texas a few years ago, there was not a fence between the Rio Grande and the north of the Panhandle, but now barbed or plain wire is the rule, and in the pastures it is of course not so necessary to look after the sheep by day and night. In Australia I have not seen those under my charge for a week or more at a time. While there was water in the paddock I never troubled even to hunt them up in the hundred square miles of grey green plain with its rare clumps of dwarf box. If dingoes were reported to be about I kept my eyes open of course, but they were very rare in the Lachlan back blocks, and I was never able to earn the five shillings reward for the tail of this yellow marauder. But in Texas, there are more wild animals, the coyote, the bear, the panther or puma, and it is impossible to leave the sheep entirely to their own devices even in pastures which prevent them wandering. Nevertheless, looking after them on fenced land is very different from being with them daily and hourly, sleeping with them at night, following and directing them by day, being all the time wary lest some should be divided from the main flock by accident, or lest the whole body should spy another sheep-owner's band and rush tumultuously into it.

But the new and unaccustomed shepherd on the prairie is apt to give himself much unnecessary trouble. It takes some time to learn that a flock of sheep is like a loosely knit organism which will not separate or divide if it can help it. It might be compared with a low kind of jelly fish, or even to a sea-anemone, for under favourable conditions of sun and sky it spreads out to feed, leaving between each of its members what is practically a constant distance. But when the weather changes they come closer together, and any alarm puts them into a compact mass. I have heard a gun fired unexpectedly, and then seen some 2,000 sheep, spreading loosely over an irregular circle about half a mile in diameter, rush for a common centre with infallible instinct. And then they gradually spread out again like that same sea-anemone putting forth its filaments after being touched.

The new shepherd, however, is in constant dread lest they should separate and divide so greatly that he will lose control of them. I have walked many useless miles endeavouring to keep a flock within unnatural limits before I discovered that they never went more than a certain distance from the centre. And this distance varied strictly with the numbers. At night time they begin to draw together, and if they are not put in a corral or fold, will at last lie down in a fairly compact mass, remaining quiet, if undisturbed, until the approach of dawn. But if they have had a bad day for feeding, they sometimes get up when the moon rises and begin to graze. Then the shepherd may wake up, and finding he is alone, have to hunt for them. As they usually feed with their heads up wind, it is not as a rule hard to discover them. If the moon is covered by a cloudy sky they will often camp down again.

The hardest days for the shepherd are cold ones, when it blows strongly. For then the sheep travel at a great pace, and will not go quietly until the sun comes out of the grey sky of the chilly norther which perhaps moderates towards noon. But in such weather they do not care to camp at noonday, and instead of spreading they will travel onward and onward. They doubtless feel uncomfortable and restless. After such a day they are uneasy at night, especially when there is a moon.

It is my opinion, after experience of both conditions, that unherded sheep do much better than those which are closely looked after. In Australia our percentage of lambs was sometimes 104, and any squatter would think something wrong if his sheep on the plain yielded less than 90 per cent. increase. But in Texas, where the mothers are watched and helped, the increase is seldom indeed 75 in the 100, much oftener it is 60. I used to wonder whether the losses by wild animals would have equalled the loss of 25 per cent. increase which is, I believe, entirely due to the care taken of them. For herding is essentially a worrying process even when practised by a man who understands sheep well. The mothers are never left alone, and must be driven to a corral at night. Consequently they often get separated from their lambs before they come to know them, and one of the most pitiful things seen by a shepherd is the poor distracted ewe refusing to recognise her own offspring even when it is shown to her. We used in such cases to put them together in a little pen during the night hoping that she would " own " it by the morning. But very often she would not, and then the lamb usually died. If, indeed, it was one of a more sturdy constitution than most, it would refuse to die and became a kind of Ishmael in the flock. The milk which was necessary it took, or tried to take, from the ewes who for just a moment might not know a stranger was trying to share the right of her own lamb. Such an orphan rarely grows up, and most of them die quickly, as they are knocked about and cruelly used by those who take no interest in the disinherited outcast of that selfish ovine society. And yet its real mother is in the flock reconciled to her loss after a few days of suffering.

In spite of my brother's very decidedly disinclination to have anything to do with sheep, they are, like every other animal, very interesting when closely studied. As he says in the text, I spent some years in their society, and knew a little about them. Shortly before he left me on Jones' ranche in North-west Texas a very curious incident occured, which I never could quite satisfactorily explain, for I believe the most serious fright I have ever had in all my life was caused by these same inoffensive, innocent quadrupeds. It was not inflicted on me by a ram, which is occasionally bellicose, but by ewes with their lambs, and I distinctly remember being as surprised as if the sky had fallen or something utterly opposed to all causation had confronted me. I want to meet a man, even of approved courage, who would not be shocked into fair fright by having half a dozen ewes suddenly turn and charge him with the fury of a bullock's mad onset. Would he not gasp, be stricken dumb, and look wild-eyed at the customary nature about him, just as if they had broken into awful speech ? I imagine he would, for I know that it shook my nerves for an hour afterwards, even though I had by that time recovered sufficient courage to experiment on them in order to see if the same result would again follow. I had about 500 ewes and lambs under my care. The day was warm, though the wind was blowing strongly, and when noon approached the flock travelled but slowly towards the place where I wished them to make their mid-day camp. To urge them on I took a long bandanna handkerchief, and flicked the nearest to me with it as I walked behind. As I did so the wind blew it strongly, and it suddenly occurred to me to make a sort of a flag of it in order to see if it would frighten them. I took hold of two corners and held it over my head, so that it might blow out to its full extent. Now, whether it was due to the glaring colour, or the strange attitude, or to the snapping of the outer edge of the handkerchief in the wind—and I think it was this last—I cannot say, but the hindmost ewes suddenly stopped, turned round, eyed me wildly, and then half a dozen made a desperate charge, struck me on the legs, threw me over, and fled precipitately as I fell. It was a reversal of experience too unexpected! I lay awhile and looked at things, expecting to see the sun blue at the least, and then I gathered myself together slowly. In all seriousness I was never so taken aback in all my life, and I was almost prepared for a ewe's biting me. I remembered the Australian story of the rich squatter catching a man killing one of his sheep. " What are you doing that for ? " he inquired, as a preliminary to requesting his company home until the police could be sent for. The questioned one looked up and answered coolly, though not, I imagine, without a twinkle in his eye. " Kill it! why am I killing it? Look here, my friend, I'll kill any man's sheep as bites *me*." For my part, I don't think biting would have alarmed me more. After that I made experiments on the ewes, and always found that the flying bandanna simply frightened them into utter desperation when nothing else would. It was a long time before they got used to it. I should like to know if any other sheep-herders ever had the same experience at home or abroad.

In another book I spoke of lambs when they were very young taking my horse for their mother. This was in California; but in Texas I have often seen them run after a bullock or steer. One day on the prairie a lamb had been born during camping-time, and when it was about two hours old a small band of cattle came down to drink at the spring. Among these was a very big steer, with horns nearly a yard long, who came close to the mother, just then engaged in cleaning her offspring. She ran off, bleating for her lamb to follow. The little chap, however, came to the conclusion that the steer was calling it, and went tottering up to the huge animal, that towered above him like the side of a cañon, apparently much to the latter's embarrassment. The steer eyed it carefully, and lifted his legs out of the way as the lamb ran against them, even backing a little, as if as surprised as I had been when the ewes assaulted me. Then all of a sudden he shook his head as if laughing, put one horn under the lamb, threw it about six feet over his back, and calmly walked on. I took it for granted that the unwary lamb was dead, but on going up I found it only stunned, and, being as yet all gristle, it soon recovered sufficiently to acknowledge its real mother, who had witnessed its sudden elevation stamping with fear and anxiety.

Sheep-herding is supposed by those who have never followed it to be an easy, idle, lazy way of procuring a livelihood; but no man who knows as much of their ways as I do will think that. It is true that there are times when there is little or nothing to be done, when a man can sit under a tree quietly and think of all the world save his own particular charge; but for the most part, if he have a conscience, he will feel a burden of responsibility upon him which of itself, independently of the work he may have to do, will earn him his little monthly wage of twenty dollars and the rough ranch food of "hog and hominy." For there is no ceasing of labour for the Texas herder of the plains; Sunday and weekday alike, the dawning sun should see him with his flock, and even at night he is still with them as they are "bedded out" in the open. Even if he can "corral" them in a rough sort of yard, some slinking coyoté may come by and scare them into breaking bounds; and when they are not corralled, the bright moon may entice them to feed quietly against the wind, until at last the herder wakes to find his charge has vanished, and must be anxiously sought for. In Australia, as I have said, the sheep are left to their own devices for the greater part of the year, unless there should be unusual scarcity of water; but, even there, to have charge of so many thousand animals and so many miles of fencing makes it no enviable task, while the labour, when it does come, is hard and unremitting. In New South Wales I have often been 18 and 20 hours in the saddle, and have reached home at last so wearied out that I could scarcely dismount. One day I used up three horses and covered over 90 miles, more than 50 of it at a hard canter or gallop—and if that be not work I should like to know what is. This, too, goes on day after day during shearing, just when the days are growing hot and hotter still, the spare herbage browning, and the water becoming scantier and scantier. And for a recompense? There is none in working with sheep. They are quiet, peaceable, stupid, illogical, incapable of exciting affection, very capable of rousing wrath; far different from the terrible excitement of a bellowing herd of long-horned cattle as they break away in a stampede, among whom is danger and sudden death and the glory of motion and conquest; or with horses thundering over the plain in hundreds, like a riderless squadron shaking the ground, with waving manes, long flowing tails, and flashing eyeballs, whom one can love and delight in, and shout to with a strange vivid joy that sends the blood tingling to the heart and brain. Were I to go back to such a life I would choose the danger, and be discontented to maunder on behind the slow and harmless wool-bearers, cursing a little every now and again at their foolishness, and then plodding on once more, bunched up in an inert mass on a slow-going horse who wearily stretches his neck almost to the ground, as he dreams, perhaps, of the long, exhilarating gallops after his own kind that we once had together, being conscious, I dare say, of the contemptuous pity I feel for the slow foredoomed muttons that crawl before us on the long and weary plain.

It is highly probable that the introduction of fences will have its effect in other ways than in increasing the number of lambs born and reared. Sheep-herding will almost disappear when the wild beasts of Texas are extinct, as they soon must be, for a fenced country is very unfit for such animals. But then the natural glory of the wide open prairie will be gone, and civilization will gradually destroy all that was so delightful, even when my sheep, by worrying me, taught me what I have here set down.

Note C.—TRAMPS, p. 170.

The poor tramp is a much abused person, and I have no doubt that he often deserves what is said of him, but, in spite of that, his life is often so hard that he might extort at the least a little sympathy—and something to eat. All Americans are too ready to

confound two distinct classes of tramps—those who take the road
to look for work, and those (the larger number, I confess) who
look for work and pray to heaven that they may never find it.
In this preponderance of the lazy traveller over the industrious lies
the distinction between the state of affairs in America and
Australia, for in the latter country the " sundowner," or
" murrumbidgee whaler," or tramp proper, is in the minority.

When I was on the tramp myself in Oregon, I was much
annoyed by being taken for one of the truly idle kind. I
remember at Roseberg, or a little to the north of it, I once
stopped and had a talk with a farmer whom I had asked for work.
Although he had none to give me, he was very civil, and we
talked of tramps and tramping. He looked at me keenly " I can
see you are not of the regular professionals," said he, " Thank you
for your perspicacity," I answered, and, though " perspicacity "
fairly floored him, he saw it was not an insult, and went on
talking. " Now look here, my boy, they say we're hard on
tramps, and perhaps some of us are, but I reckon we sometimes
get enough to make us rough. Last summer I was in my orchard,
picking cherries, I think, and a likely-looking, strong young fellow
comes along the road. Seeing me, he climbs the fence, and says
to me, ' Say, boss, could you give me something to eat ? I haven't
had anything to-day.' I looked at him. ' Why, yes,' said I, ' If
you'll go up to the house. I'll be up there in a few minutes,
when I've filled this pail; and while you're waiting just split a
little wood. The axe is on the wood pile.' Now, look you, what
d'ye think he said. ' I don't split wood. I an't going to do any
work till I get to Washington Territory.' ' Oh !' said I, ' that's it,
is it ? Then look here, young fellow, don't you eat anything, till
you get there either ; for I won't give you anything, and just let
me see you climb that fence in a hurry.' So he went off cursing.
Ain't that kind of thing enough to make us rough on tramps ? let
alone that they steal the chickens ; and if you look as you go down
the road, you'll see feathers by every place they camp." That was
true enough, and south of the Umpqua I used to find goose
feathers every few hundred yards. On that same tramp down
through Oregon, I once met four men travelling north. There
had been a murder committed by a tramp to the south of Roseberg, and we stopped under an old scrubby oak to talk it over.
Three of them were working men, but the fourth was a true

professional, about 50 years of age, whose clothes were ragged to the last extremity of tatters. His hands were brown at the backs, but I noticed, when I gave him some tobacco, which he very promptly asked for, that the palms were perfectly soft. He told us how long he had travelled, and how many years it was since he had done any work ; and, finally rising, he picked up a wretched-looking blanket, and said, " Well, good day, gentlemen. I'm off to call on the mayor of Portland and a few rich friends of mine up there." He winked good-humouredly and shambled off.

I met a lame young fellow near Jacksonville, who told me he had come all the way from New York State, and was thinking of going back. He was in very good spirits, and did not appear in the least dismayed at the prospect of tramping 2,000 miles, for he was one of those who do not use the railroad and " beat their way." When I was at work in Sonoma County, California, a little fellow came and worked for 10 days, who once travelled 200 miles inside the cowcatcher of an engine. Most English people know the wedge-shaped pilot in front of the American engine well enough by repute to recognise it. When the engine was in the yard over the hollow track he crawled in, taking a board to sit on inside. When the locomotive once ran out on the ordinary track it was impossible to remove him, although the fireman soon discovered his presence there, and poured some warm water over him. On coming to a little town about fifty miles from his destination, the constable came down to the train. " He came," said Hub (that was our tramp's name), " to see that no tramps got off there, or, if they did, to advise them to clear out. He walked to the engine and said ' Good day ' to the driver. ' Got any tramps on board to-day, Jack ? ' he said. ' We've got one,' he answered ; ' but we can't get him off.' ' Why ? how's that ? ' said the constable. ' Go and look at the pilot.' So he came round and looked at me, and he burst into a laugh. ' All right, Jack,' says he ; ' you can keep him. He won't trouble us, I can see.' And with that he poked me with his stick, and called everyone to take a look. I said nothing, but you bet I felt mean to be cooped up there, not able to move, with all the folks laughing at me."

But, in spite of Hub's sad experiences, he went off on the tramp again as soon as he had enough to buy a pair of new boots with.

Tramps—that is, the bad ones among them—are very often
insolent when they find no one but women in a house. Once
a man I knew was working in Indiana, but, having a bad headache, he remained in one morning. By-and-by a truculent looking
tramp came along. "Kin you give us suthin' to eat, ma'am?" he
growled. "Certainly," said the woman, who was always kind to
travellers. She set about making him a meal, and put out some
bread and meat. The tramp, who certainly did not look hungry,
eyed it with disfavour. "Bah!" said he at last, with intense
contempt; "I don't want that stuff. D'ye think I'm starving?
An't you got suthing nice—say, some strawberry shortcake and
cream?" The woman stared with astonishment, as well she
might. But the man with the headache heard Mr. Tramp's
remarks. There was a shot gun hanging in the room where he
was; so, slipping off the bed, he reached for the weapon, walked
out quietly, and, thrusting the muzzle of the gun under the tramp's
ear, he roared in a fierce voice "Get!" And, to use the
vernacular, the tramp "got" instantly.

The last story I will tell of tramps is perhaps the most audacious
of all. I met the chief actor in British Columbia. It appears
that he and another man went one Sunday to a very respectable
farmhouse in Illinois to beg for food. They knocked, and there
was no answer. They knocked again, and still without avail.
Then they opened the unlocked door and went in. The dining
table was laid ready for a feast, as it seemed, for it was adorned
with an admirable cold collation, including a turkey, several fowls,
and a number of pies. The eyes of my acquaintance and his
partner sparkled. Here was a chance, for the family was at
church. They went out, got a sack, and hastily tumbled into it
the turkey, the fowls, some bread, and the most substantial pies.
Just as it was getting full one looked out of the window, and saw
a man coming up the path. They were struck with terror of
discovery, but, on watching, they soon saw that this was a tramp
like themselves. He came up, and knocked at the door. "Can
you give me something to eat, sir?" he asked humbly. "I guess
so," said my acquaintance coolly; "that is, if you ain't one of the
tramps that won't work. Will you cut some wood for your
dinner?" "Of course I will," said the tramp gladly; and he
went to the wood pile. While he was at work the two spoilers of
the Egyptians departed through the back door, and went about

a hundred yards to the corner of a wood, where they laughed till they cried. The result of their manœuvre was sure to be too good to be lost, so one of them climbed up a tree and watched. In about a quarter of an hour he saw a string of men and women coming towards the house, and still the working tramp made the chips fly. On entering the yard, one of the men went up to interview him, and, by the tramp's gestures, it was evident he was explaining that he had been set to work. Meanwhile the women went in, but came out again in a moment, shrieking with indigna· tion. The next sight was the farmer, armed with a stick, belabouring the astonished worker, who fled across the fence incontinently. He was followed to the very verge of the wood, and then the exhausted "mossback" left him to return to the house. "It was just the funniest thing I ever saw," declared my unabashed friend; "and to see that poor fellow get whipped for our sins nearly killed me. But I tell you, we rewarded him for his labour after all. We found him sitting on a stump, rubbing himself all over, and invited him to dinner with us. So, you see, he got the grub we promised him, and he didn't work for nothing; for that would just kill a tramp."

Note D.—RAILROAD WARS, p. 194.

Everybody nowadays has some notion of the way the railroad business of America is carried on. They know that there are too many roads for the traffic, and that, to prevent a general ruin, the managers combine, pay the profits into the hands of a receiver, and receive again from him a certain agreed proportion of the whole sum. But this method of "pooling" the profits is some-times unsatisfactory. One line will think it gets too little if the fluctuations of trade send more freight over its rails than it formerly had, and will demand a greater proportion of the gross profits. This demand may be granted, but if not the agreement may break down, and the discontented railroad go to work on the old principle of every man for himself. This very likely inaugurates a war of tariffs; fares and freights go down slowly or quickly according as the quarrel is open or secret, until one or other of the parties to the quarrel gives in to avoid complete ruin.

While I was living in San Francisco, early in 1886, there was an open war between all the lines west of Chicago and Kansas City, including the Union Pacific, the Northern Pacific, the Denver and Rio Grande, the Southern Pacific, and the Atchison, Topeka, and Santa Fé. Fares to New York and the Atlantic seaboard came tumbling down by $10 at a fall. The usual rate to New York from San Francisco is $72. It fell to 60, to 50, 40, 30, to 25, to 22. All the railroad offices had great placards outside inviting everyone to go east at once, for they would never get such a chance again. Some of the notices were very odd. One began with "Blood, blood, blood!" and another had a hand holding a bowie knife, with the legend "Here we cut deep!" And, as I have said, they did cut deep, for at the end one might go to New York for about $18. Now this $18 went in a lump to the railroad east of Chicago. Consequently the passengers were carried over 2,000 miles for nothing. Frequently during two days men were booked to Chicago or Kansas City from San Francisco or Los Angeles for $1. Two thousand miles for 4s. 2d.

Such a state of things could not last, but while it did it gave rise to much speculation. Many men bought up tickets, good for some time, believing the bottom prices had been reached when the fall had by no means ended. It was odd to stand outside an office and listen to the crowd. Some would hold on and say, "I'll chance it till to-morrow." Then I have seen an agent come outside and say, "Gentlemen, now's your time to go east and visit your families. Don't delay. Of course fares may fall further, but I think not. Don't be too greedy. You are not likely to get the chance again of going home for twenty-five dollars." They did fall further, but recovered again on the rumour of negotiations beginning between the competing lines. When that was contradicted they fell again. Suddenly, without any warning, they jumped up to normal rates, and left many of the outside public—the bears, so to speak—lamenting that they had not taken the opportunity so eloquently pointed out by the oratorical agents on the sidewalk by the offices. For the placards and pictures came down at once, and to an inquirer who asked, "What can you do New York at?" the answer was, "Why, sir, the usual rate, $72."

To an Englishman who has not travelled in the States and become familiar with the methods employed there by business men, it seems odd that any one should chaffer with the clerk at a ticket office. What would an English booking clerk say if he were asked about the fare to some place, and, in replying £1, received the rejoinder, " I'll give you 15s."? He would think the man a joker of a very feeble description. Yet this may often be done in Western America. Even when there is no "war" on, the agents have a certain margin to veer and haul on in their commission, and will often knock off a little sooner than allow a rival line to get the passenger. Besides, it frequently happens that there may be a secret cutting of rates without an open war. My own experience, when I came down from Sonoma County in the autumn of 1886, meaning to return to England, will give a very good notion of this, and of the way to get a cheap ticket when there is the trouble among the companies which may end in a war, or be patched up by arbitration.

It had been said in the papers for some time that rate cutting was going on in San Francisco, and this made me hurry down not to lose the opportunity. The morning after my arrival I walked into an office in Kearney Street, and said briefly, " What are you doing to New York?" The clerk said in a business way, " Seventy-two dollars." I laughed a little, and looked at him straight without speaking. " Hum," said he; " well you can go for sixty-five." " Thanks," I said : " it isn't enough." I walked out, and though he called me back I would not return. Then I went to Mr. P., a well-known agent for railroads and steamships. To use a vulgarism, he did not open his mouth so wide as the other, but at once offered me a through ticket to Liverpool for $72. I thanked him, and said I would call again. Deducting the $12 for a steerage passage, his railroad fare was $60. So far I had knocked off $12. And now it began to rain very hard. It did not cease all day. And my day's work was only begun, for it was only ten o'clock then. I went from one office to another, quoting one's rates here and another's there, and slowly I dropped the fare to fifty. I had to explain to some of these men that I was not a fool, and that I knew what I was doing; that if they took me for a "tenderfoot" or a " sucker" they were mistaken. My explanations always had an effect, and down the fare tumbled. At last, about three o'clock, I had got things to a very fine point, and was working two rival offices which stood side by side near the Palace Hotel. One man—Mr. A., whom I knew by name, who indeed knew a friend of mine—offered me $45. I shook my head, and, going next door, Mr. V. gave me a dollar less. It took me half an hour to reduce that again to forty-three; but at last Mr. A., who was as much interested in this little game as if I were a big stake at poker, went suddenly down to $41. I offered to toss him whether it should be $40 or $42. He accepted, and I won the toss. As he made out the ticket, he remarked, almost sadly, "We don't make anything out of this." But he cheered up, and added, "Well, the others don't either." So I got my ticket; and it was over one of the best lines. By that day's work, though I got wet through, covered with mud, and very tired, I saved $32.

When on board the east-bound train next day, I got talking with some dozen men who were going east with me, and, naturally enough, we asked each other what fares we had paid. I found they varied greatly, but the average was about $60. One little Jew, a tobacconist, was very proud that his only cost $48. He almost wept when I told him that I beat him by eight whole dollars. Moreover, I reached New York twenty hours before him, for when we parted at Chicago we made arrangements to meet in New York, and then I found that he had been obliged to go round into Canada, and lie over all one night, while I had come direct on the Chicago and Alton with only two hours' wait at Lima; so on the whole I do not think I did very badly.

Note E.—AMERICAN SHIPMASTERS, p. 232.

It may seem strange to people who are entirely unacquainted with the methods of shipmasters and officers generally in the American mercantile marine that a sailor should have such a deadly objection to sail in one of their vessels; but those who know the hideous brutalities which continually occur on such ships will quite understand the feelings of a man who finds himself on a vessel which would probably have been manned willingly if it had not a bad character among seamen. I have known an American vessel lie six weeks and more off Sandridge, Melbourne, waiting for a crew, which she could not get, although men were very plentiful and the boarding-houses full. There are some vessels running from New York, &c. round the Horn to San Francisco which have a villainous reputation. The captain of one of these was sentenced to 18 months in the Penitentiary when I was in the great Pacific port for incredible atrocities practised on his crew. For one thing, he shot repeatedly at men who were up aloft, and hit one of them who was on the main-yard, though not so seriously as to make him quit his hold of the jack-stay. One of the ship's boys was treated with barbarity during the whole passage; thrashed, beaten, starved, and ill-used in the vilest manner; and at last the captain knocked him down and jumped on his face so as to blind him for life. This man went a little too far, and the courts which are always biassed, and very naturally biassed considering their origin, on the side of rich authority, were compelled to do their duty by the uproar that this last incident caused. Yet even after that the people connected with the shipping interests got up petitions and intrigued and wire-pulled for months to get the Governor of California to pardon him. Failing in this, they approached the President; but I am heartily glad their efforts were vain.

One of my own shipmates on the Coloma, of Portland, Oregon, was once with a commander of this class, and so bad was his reputation that no one among the crew knew until they were under way who the captain was. My mate said, "I was at the wheel when I saw him come up the companion, and, as I had sailed with him before, my blood ran cold when I recognised him. He came straight up to the wheel, stared at me, and asked me, 'Haven't you sailed with me before?' 'Yes, sir,' I answered. Then he grinned, 'Ha, then you know me. When you go forward you tell the men what kind of a captain I am, and tell them that if they behave themselves I'll be a father to 'em.' I knew what his being a father to us meant. However, I didn't see any good in scaring the fellows, so when my trick was over I told them the skipper was a real beauty. Just then there was a roar from the poop, 'Relieve the wheel;' and the man who had relieved me came staggering forrard with his face smothered in blood. He had let her run off a quarter of a point or so, and the skipper, without saying a word, struck him right between the eyes with the end of his brass telescope, cutting his nose and forehead in great gashes. That was his way of being a father to us, and he kept it up all the passage. The first chance I got I skinned out!"

It is true that the American mercantile marine is not so bad as it was. These things do not occur in all vessels, but even yet they occur so frequently that an English sailor would as a general rule rather sail with the devil himself than with an American skipper. What the state of affairs was some 20 or 30 years ago one can hardly imagine, but it certainly was much worse then. Shanghai-ing is not so much practised. There is a story current among seamen, though I know not how true it is, that it was checked owing to the lieutenant of an English man-of-war being drugged and carried on board an American merchantman. However, there is now, or was but lately, a boarding-house keeper in San Francisco, whose christian or first name had been abolished in favour of " Shanghai." I had the very doubtful honour of knowing him, and could easily believe any stories told of his chicanery and treachery to sailormen.